IT'S PIN
BIN DIM
DOMINILLI!

Books by Cormac MacRaois

The Battle Below Giltspur

Dance of the Midnight Fire

Lightning over Giltspur

Cormac Mac Raois

WOLFHOUND PRESS

Reprinted 1994

First published 1993 by
WOLFHOUND PRESS
68 Mountjoy Square
Dublin 1

Wolfhound Press receives financial assistance from the Arts Council / An Chomhairle Ealaíon, Dublin, Ireland.

This book is fiction. All characters, incidents and names have no connection with any persons living or dead. Any apparent resemblance is purely coincidental.

British Library Cataloguing in Publication Data

Mac Raois, Cormac
  It's Pin-bin-dim-dominilli
  I. Title II. White, Katharine
  823.914 [J]

  ISBN 0-86327-408-0

Cover and text illustration: Katharine White
Typesetting: Wolfhound Press
Printed by The Guernsey Press Co. Ltd., Guernsey, Channel Islands.

CONTENTS

For my nephew
Christopher O Connor

1   Pin

Jim heard Pin before he saw him. He was giving out, of course. Even though Jim couldn't see him, Pin's voice sounded clearly in his head. That was hardly surprising as he was sitting on the pillow right beside his ear.

'I always get left behind,' grumbled the slightly hoarse voice. 'No one ever waits for me. It's not fair. I'm all alone and cold. Atishoo-yek!'

The sneeze was a remarkable explosion with a hiccup on its tail.

Jim was surprised of course. You don't expect to hear a strange voice in your ear first thing on a Saturday morning, especially when you have a bedroom all to yourself. He opened one eye. A pale light showed behind the closed curtains. The air in the room was chilly. He didn't want to struggle up from under the warm bedclothes yet. Perhaps the voice had been part of a dream.

'It's such a sleepy head! You'd think it would waken up

for breakfast. I can't wait all day. Atishoo-yek!'

Jim heaved himself up in the bed and leaning on his elbow, reached over and switched on the light.

'Yah!' yelled the voice, startling him. He looked all around but he still couldn't see anyone.

'Who's there?' he demanded, beginning to feel nervous.

'You big clumsy lout!' roared the voice. 'Why can't you mind what you're doing?'

'Where are you?' Jim shouted back, feeling both alarmed and annoyed.

'I'm hanging on the edge of this cliff!' raged the voice. 'Are you blind as well as stupid?'

'Cliff?' muttered Jim. 'What cliff?'

Then he saw a pair of tiny brown hands gripping the edge of the white sheet. His heart gave a sudden thud and his stomach went 'Wow!' He leaned over to see who was there but as he did, the mattress moved and the hands lost their grip. There was a soft thump on the floor, then that voice again.

'You big bully! You dirty rotten bully!' He sounded as if he was having a tantrum.

Jim peeped over the edge of the bed and saw a tiny little man — about fifteen centimetres tall — sitting on the floor. He was wearing a floppy brown leather hat with a wide brim that hid his face and a mustard-coloured jacket and trousers, made of some sort of animal skin. He had a red shirt with golden buttons down the front and dark brown leather boots.

Jim gazed at him with a mixture of delight and wonder. Then the little man looked up and Jim saw a sun-tanned wrinkled face with mischief written in every line. Fury flashed from the most intense pair of eyes Jim had ever seen. He squinted up at Jim. Then he puffed out his cheeks in frustration and thumped the carpet with his small fist.

'Bah!' was all he could think of saying.

'Who are you?' Jim asked. 'And what are you doing in my bedroom?'

'I'm Pinbindimdominilli,' he replied raising his hat with a dramatic flourish, to reveal a head of tight brown curly hair. 'As for what I'm doing in your bedroom, I should have thought it was obvious that I'm sitting on your floor.'

'Pin-bi-dom-' began Jim but he couldn't remember the rest.

'Pin-bin-dim-dom-in-illi,' declared the stranger, thumping the floor at each part of his name and ending with a sigh of enormous patience.

'Pinbindimdominilli,' repeated Jim, just to prove he wasn't as stupid as the little man thought. 'That's an enormous name for such a tiny person.'

Pin jammed his hat back on his head and leaped to his feet with surprising speed. 'What's your name?' he demanded.

'Jim,' replied Jim, slightly taken aback by Pin's forcefulness.

'Humph!' he grunted. 'That's a tiny name for such an enormous person.'

'I'm not enormous for a boy,' Jim replied. 'In fact I'm rather small.'

'And I'm not tiny for a Dominillo,' Pin retorted. 'In fact I'm rather tall.'

'Are you a leprechaun?' asked Jim.

A look of horror spread over Pin's face. 'Are you stone deaf?' he growled.

'Of course not,' answered Jim. 'I just asked if you were a lep —'

'And I just told you I'm a Dominillo, not one of those other things,' snapped Pin.

'Sorry if I insulted you,' murmured Jim.

'So you should be,' grumbled Pin.

With that he caught hold of the edge of the sheet and climbed up onto the bed. As Jim was lying down, Pin was able to look him straight in the face. 'That's better,' he sighed, obviously satisfied that they were on even terms. 'How old are you, young giant?'

'Young giant!' exclaimed Jim. That would be a fine thing! Jim was the smallest in his class. The lads all called him Tinchy and they weren't shy about showing off their superior physical strength by knocking him about every now and then.

'I'm ten but I'll be eleven tomorrow. It's my birthday.'

Pin gave a start and stared open-mouthed at Jim. Then his face flushed red. 'You're a liar!' he exploded.

'I am not!' Jim retorted indignantly. 'How dare you call me a liar, you little squirt!'

'I'm not a little squirt!' fumed Pin. 'And it's *my* birthday tomorrow. How dare you steal my birthday!'

'I didn't steal it,' protested Jim. 'It's my birthday. I was born on the eleventh of November and I'll be eleven tomorrow, so there!'

Pin stared hard at him for a moment, then he drew himself up to his full height. 'I'll be a hundred and twenty one,' he boasted.

'A hundred and twenty one!' exclaimed Jim. 'How can anyone so small be so old?'

'How can anyone so big be so young?' replied Pin.

'You're impossible!' declared Jim.

'So are you,' retorted Pin.

Just as the conversation ground to a halt, the doorhandle rattled and Jim's sister Caitríona barged in without knocking, as usual. Caitríona was Jim's twin, and had blue eyes and shoulder-length black hair that she wore in a pony-tail. Jim called her Cat for short. Caitríona hated being called that, so Jim enjoyed using it all the more.

The instant the door creaked open, Pin did an incredible cartwheel across the bed and vanished under the duvet.

'Who were you talking to?' demanded Caitríona.

It was obvious that Pin didn't want anyone else to see him and Jim certainly wasn't going to let Caitríona bully her way into his secret.

'No one,' he replied, lying back on his pillow and closing his eyes in mock boredom.

'Liar!' she accused. 'I was outside the door and I heard voices.'

Sneaky sister, thought Jim. This was the second time that morning he'd been called a liar and he hadn't even had breakfast yet. Then he realised that he didn't need to lie to Caitríona. The truth would do the trick beautifully.

'All right,' he sighed. 'I'll tell you.'

A look of superior-sister triumph spread across Caitríona's face, but it didn't bother Jim as much as usual. He knew he would soon have the pleasure of wiping it off again.

'If you must know,' he drawled, enjoying the moment, 'I was talking to a little man about fifteen centimetres tall. He wears a suit of mustard-coloured animal skin, a red shirt with golden buttons, a brown wide-brimmed hat and leather boots. I've decided to call him Pin, though he tells me his real name is Pinbindimdominilli. Satisfied?'

'Very funny,' declared Caitríona, trying to wither him with a look of scorn. 'Really Jim, you're so childish.' Then with a toss of her long black hair, she flounced out of the bedroom, slamming the door.

'You can come out now, Pin,' sighed Jim. He had a feeling that this was going to be a rather tricky day.

A small bump under the duvet stirred, then moved towards

the pillow. Pin's head peeped out. He didn't look very pleased.

'What did you do that for?' he demanded.

'Do what?' Jim asked innocently.

'Tell her about me, you numbskull!'

'It was perfectly safe,' Jim replied calmly.

'Safe!' squeaked Pin. 'Sisters are never safe.'

'Hmm,' said Jim. 'You may be right about that, but in this case I'm a step ahead of both of you.'

'How?' asked Pin as he climbed up onto the headboard.

'She still doesn't know about you,' answered Jim.

'Doesn't know!' gasped Pin, staring at Jim as if he was now certain that he'd taken up with a complete lunatic. 'Of course she knows. You've just told her — or have you forgotten already?'

Jim ignored the sarcasm in his voice and with all the dignity of a misunderstood genius, he began to explain. 'She doesn't know because she doesn't believe. As far as she's concerned, you don't exist. The more I tell her about you the more convinced she'll be that I'm making it all up. Before long, she'll be so annoyed with me that even if she saw you with her own two eyes she wouldn't believe you were real. Now you couldn't be safer than that, could you? And I won't have to keep on telling lies about you either.'

Pin looked at Jim with a new respect. 'Very crafty,' he murmured. He laughed softly to himself, then leaped off the headboard, did a mid-air somersault and landed on his bottom on the pillow.

'You're really brilliant at that,' remarked Jim.

'And you're a very clever young giant,' replied Pin, giving Jim a broad grin followed by a friendly punch on the shoulder.

Then they both laughed.

'Where do you come from?' Jim asked. It seemed a reasonable question but Pin's laughter died suddenly and he looked cranky again. He didn't reply.

'Come on,' coaxed Jim. 'You can tell me. I'm your friend.'

Pin looked so much like a sulky child that Jim almost laughed out loud at him, but he held it in, guessing that Pin would be highly insulted.

'I can't remember,' mumbled Pin, looking away.

'Don't be ridiculous,' Jim protested. 'Everyone knows where they come from.'

'Well I don't!' snapped Pin.

'How did you get here?' Jim insisted.

'I don't remember,' muttered Pin.

'You sound just like the home-work dodgers in my class,' said Jim. 'When they can't think of an excuse for not doing their work they say "I forgot" as if anyone ever forgets homework.'

'What's homework?' asked Pin.

'Homework! Don't you have schools in — wherever you come from?'

Pin rolled his eyes and sighed heavily. 'What are schools?'

'You've no schools!' exclaimed Jim.

'If we had I'd hardly ask you what they were, would I?' growled Pin.

'I suppose not,' Jim admitted. 'Schools are great big buildings where hundreds of children are kept sitting down all day listening to adults telling them things they don't want to know and giving out to them because they won't sit still and stay quiet and listen — and even when the children *are* let out again, they have to write things out at home about the stuff the adults were explaining — that's what we call homework — and if you don't do the homework you get into trouble with the grown-ups.'

Pin looked horrified. 'Sounds like the Nelligenti Reformatory,' he muttered.

'The what?' asked Jim.

'Oh, nothing,' Pin flustered. 'Do you have to go to school?'

'Of course.'

'You must have done something dreadful to be sent there,' said Pin, gazing at Jim with a mixture of admiration and unease, as if he'd discovered he was a dangerous and daring criminal.

'Don't be silly,' laughed Jim. 'Everyone has to go there. Their parents make them go.'

'Your parents must be very cruel people,' sighed Pin sadly.

'It's not their fault,' explained Jim. 'It's the law. Anyway, they only send us so we can learn lots of things and pass tests and get good jobs and be rich when we grow up.'

Pin looked puzzled.

'Don't worry,' smiled Jim. 'It's not as bad as it sounds. The teachers aren't as much of a problem as the other children. There are nearly five hundred pupils in our school and it's hard going to survive in the crowd.'

'I can well imagine,' agreed Pin glumly.

'Are you hungry?' asked Jim, wanting to get away from the subject of school.

'Starving,' admitted Pin.

'Right,' said Jim, sliding out onto the floor. 'It's time we got some breakfast.'

He put on his slippers and the red dressing-gown his gran had given him for Christmas. After a brief argument, Pin agreed to be carried in one of the deep pockets. And so, humming innocently, Jim brought Pin down to the kitchen for breakfast.

&

'What are you so cheerful about?' demanded Eileen, Jim's big sister. Eileen was seventeen and usually a bit grumpy at breakfast.

'Pardon?' mumbled Jim through his cornflakes. Eileen had just disturbed a very interesting daydream about a game of table-football played by a team of Dominilli.

'You were humming happily to yourself with a big grin on your face,' said Eileen. 'You've been told not to hum at the table.'

'Oh,' replied Jim, as he sneaked another dry cornflake from the edge of his bowl and slipped it into the pocket of his dressing-gown where he could feel Pin taking it from him. 'It's Saturday, isn't it? There's no school and tomorrow's my birthday, so why shouldn't I be in good humour?'

'He's up to something,' accused Caitríona. 'He always hums when he's planning something.'

Jim hated her for knowing him so well. 'I'd rather hum than nag like you two old spotty-faced witches,' he retorted.

That really got them going. Caitríona began shouting abuse. Eileen hit him with a dishcloth and knocked over the milk-jug in the process. Then their mother burst into the kitchen.

Mary Doran was a kind and generally patient person but there were times when her children's ability to make a row out of everything strained her good nature to breaking point.

'What's wrong with the three of you now?' she demanded.

'He called us spotty old witches,' complained Eileen.

'And he won't stop humming,' added Caitríona, determined to get her bit in. She enjoyed getting Jim into trouble.

'I wasn't doing anything,' protested Jim. 'And *I* didn't spill the milk,' he added, glaring meaningfully at Eileen.

Mrs Doran raised her eyes to the ceiling as if there was a witness up there who could see what she had to put up with. 'Why can't you three just have your breakfast without always bickering?' she sighed.

'May I have some toast?' asked Jim, wanting to head-off another of Mam's long sermons about her impossible children.

'Oh, go on,' she replied. 'Just keep an eye on it so it doesn't get burnt.'

The electric toaster, like a lot of odds and ends in the Dorans' house, didn't work properly. It toasted the bread all right but it wouldn't pop up, so if you forgot to pull the lever you ended up with cinder-toast and a smoky kitchen.

As he'd had enough trouble for one breakfast, Jim stood over the toast until it was ready. When he was safely back at the table and shielded from the glaring faces of his sisters, he slipped a piece of broken crust into his pocket and felt Pin stand up and reach for it. Soon a series of tiny crunches told him that Pin was enjoying his toast. The others didn't notice the sound because Jim began munching his own food deliberately loudly.

'Do you have to make so much noise?' moaned Eileen, with a look of disgust on her face.

'Yes,' replied Jim truthfully enough and he grinned at her. He was congratulating himself on a fairly successful breakfast, when a loud miaow from beneath the table alerted him to a problem he'd overlooked.

Matsa, the family cat, had spotted the movement in his dressing-gown pocket. Now she was standing on her hind legs with her front paws on the chair and her head stretched up as she sniffed at him.

Normally Jim was quite fond of Matsa. He loved her mixture of pure white hair and the patches of black and grey on her sides and between her ears. She was also highly intelligent. However, this was not the right moment for her to be clever. He looked coldly into her bright green eyes and whispered 'Rottweiler!' She blinked coolly at him, miaowed loudly again and poked at his pocket with her paw.

'What's the matter with that cat?' asked Mrs Doran as she poured boiling water into the teapot. 'Does she need to go out?'

'It's something in Jim's pocket!' Caitríona shouted helpfully.

Deciding it was time to go, Jim stuffed the rest of the toast into his mouth and stood up from the table. Matsa leaped onto his chair and tried to get at his pocket again.

'Look at that!' exclaimed Eileen. 'What have you got in there — a dead fish?'

'It's a dirty sock,' lied Jim as he helped Matsa off the chair with the back of his hand.

'Probably smells like a fish,' jeered Caitríona.

'I'll put it in the wash-basket,' mumbled Jim as he hurried towards the door.

'Speaking of washing,' said his Mam, 'you're due a bath. Go and have it now.'

'OK,' replied Jim as he skipped out of the kitchen and sprinted upstairs.

2   In Hot Water

Usually Jim wasn't all that keen on baths, but he was glad enough to lock the bathroom door behind him and be assured of half-an-hour to himself away from prying eyes.

Pin's head popped out of his pocket. He had a grin on his face and toast-crumbs on his hat.

'Thanks for the breakfast,' he said.

'Thanks for the trouble,' Jim answered sourly.

'I enjoyed both,' Pin chirped cheekily and burst into a fit of giggles.

'I think you're going to be a nuisance,' sighed Jim but he had to smile at the little man. 'Hold on tightly,' he warned as he slipped off his dressing-gown and hung it on the back of the door. Pin really looked comical peeping out of his pocket with his little hat perched crookedly on his head.

Jim began to run the bath water.

'Oh goody!' exclaimed Pin. 'A swimming pool!'

'It's a bath,' Jim corrected him, as he went to the sink and began to squeeze toothpaste onto his toothbrush.

Pin hoisted himself out of the pocket and gripping the material of the dressing-gown, climbed down to the hem. Then he dropped lightly to the floor.

'It's just like the pool in Bendovina Falls,' said Pin, 'all whirlpools and splashings and waves and...' He was bubbling with excitement. Then he realised that Jim was listening intently and he stopped short.

Jim was getting used to these sudden endings. Every time Pin was about to give away some piece of personal information, he would stop himself just in time. Jim felt sure his visitor wouldn't be able to keep on being so cautious. Sooner or later he was going to slip up. He decided not to press him. He was more likely to give information away when he was relaxed. Jim began to scrub his teeth as if nothing had happened.

Pin stood watching him for a moment. The sight of a 'giant' brushing his teeth was something worth looking at. Then he hopped onto the weighing scales, which didn't register any weight for him at all and from there he was able to leap up and grip the edge of the bath. He drew himself up to the rim, just like an athlete doing chin-ups on the bars in a gymnasium.

Jim really had to admire Pin's agility. Physical education was not his favourite school activity. After one chin-up his arms felt like cooked spaghetti and he just dangled in mid-air till he eventually had to let go and fall to the floor in embarrassment with the whole class watching.

Pin had no such problem. He swung himself up onto the rim and sat with his feet dangling above the steaming water. Then he stood up and calmly walked along the edge until he was beside Jim. He hopped up onto the towel rail and from there to the sink. He began examining the toothpaste tube which was almost the same size as himself. Looking at him,

Jim felt that the bathroom was going to be one of Pin's favourite places.

'You really are a brilliant athlete, Pin,' he remarked innocently. 'Are all the Dominilli as nimble as you?'

'The young ones aren't,' replied Pin, glowing with self-satisfaction. 'But we all practise for years at the Bendovina Woods. The trees there are...'

He stopped again and glared at Jim. 'You sly trickster,' he growled. 'I'll get you for that.'

Jim laughed at him, hung up his toothbrush and went to turn off the bath taps. Then he slipped off his pyjamas and dipped one foot in the water to test the temperature.

Suddenly Eileen's voice said very loudly, 'Jim! You've got a huge backside!'

Jim nearly leaped out of his bare skin. He grabbed at a towel to cover himself, trying at the same time to hop back from the bath, but he lost his balance and fell against the radiator. As he lay there in stunned confusion, he looked up, expecting to see Eileen somehow standing beside the sink. She wasn't there of course. How could she be? What he saw was Pin collapsing in a fit of uncontrollable laughter. The little rascal sat on the toothpaste tube as tears streamed down his face. Then he rolled backwards and kicked his legs in the air, all the while laughing his tiny head off. 'Got you!' he squeaked breathlessly.

'You little horror!' exclaimed Jim, as he scrambled to his feet. 'How on earth did you do that? You sounded just like Eileen.'

'I've always been able to copy voices,' replied Pin.

'But you spoke so loudly,' objected Jim, even now unable to believe that the sound had come from the tiny man on the sink.

'That's part of our training in the Mirandelli Theatre. I'm

one of the best. In fact I — '

'What are you doing in there?' demanded Mr Doran's deep voice from the other side of the door. This time it wasn't Pin being smart.

'I-I'm getting ready to have a bath,' Jim replied.

'What's all the noise about?' said Jim's Dad. 'You'd think there were three of you in there.'

'I lost my balance when I was getting in,' Jim answered half-truthfully.

'Why were you talking to yourself?' insisted his father.

Jim couldn't think of an answer to that one. Then he heard his own voice saying, 'I was practising a play we're doing in school.' Pin was at it again. Jim glared at him and shook his fist. Pin held up his hands as if to say 'I'm only doing my best.'

'Get on with your bath,' grumbled Mr Doran. 'Other people need to get in there too, you know.'

'Very clever, Pin,' Jim growled as he stepped into the bath. 'You'll do that once too often.'

'It worked, didn't it?' Pin replied airily.

Jim lay back letting the lovely warm water come right up to his ears. 'Anyway, my bottom isn't huge.'

'It's the biggest one I've ever seen,' smirked Pin.

'It's exactly right for me,' Jim replied. 'I'd look a right twerp if I had a puny little pea-botty like yours.'

Pin didn't bother to reply to that, but stood up and began walking on the toothpaste tube. 'Wow! This is a lovely feeling,' he cried as the tube yielded slowly beneath his feet. 'I really fancy this.' He began prancing about on it, leaping into the air and doing fancy landings like a ballet dancer.

Jim started to soap himself and didn't pay much more attention to Pin until he heard him mutter 'Ooops!' Then he glanced up.

Jim's mother was always nagging him about leaving the

top off the toothpaste. This was one occasion when he wished
he'd heeded her. Pin's antics had sent the toothpaste flying
out of the tube in a series of squirts and blobs. Now a sticky
white worm oozed down the side of the handbasin, there was
a heap of white goo on the green carpet and even some spots
on the pink curtains by the window.

'Pin, you fool!' shouted Jim. 'Look what you've done!'

'Oh-oh. Sorry,' said Pin.

By the sound of his voice, Jim reckoned he'd often been
guilty of causing similar messes. 'Mam will kill me,' he
hissed. 'And you've used up almost all of a new tube of
toothpaste.'

'Relax,' said Pin. 'I'll clean it up.'

'You'd better,' threatened Jim.

He should have had more sense. While he was shampoo-
ing his hair, Pin got across onto the toilet seat, dived onto the
toilet roll and sailed down to the floor pulling the roll of paper
out after him. Then he stood on a square of it and tore it along
the perforations. Armed with this he began to 'clean up'. By
the time Jim had rinsed the shampoo out of his hair and the
soap out of his eyes, the carpet was smeared with streaks of
white toothpaste decorated with shreds of pink toilet roll, the
sink looked as if someone had been trying to paint it white
and the pink curtains looked like a snow-storm. Pin was
standing in the sink quite pleased with himself.

'Oh no,' groaned Jim. 'Pin, you bloomin' idiot!'

He hopped out of the bath and reached out to grab the little
man. Pin slipped through his wet fingers and leaped from the
sink onto the windowsill where he collided with a box of talc.
As the talc tumbled to the floor, the top shot off and the fine
white powder spewed out all over the carpet. A cloud of
fragrant dust floated up into the air and Pin sneezed explo-
sively.

'I'm going to kill you,' Jim growled, reaching for him.

'Jim! What's going on in there? Open this door at once.'

It was Mam. Now he was really in trouble. There was no arguing with that tone of voice. He pulled on his dressing gown and turned to grab Pin but he had vanished.

'Open this door at once!' thundered Mam.

Reluctantly Jim unlocked the door. Mam strode in. She took one look at the mess, then she exploded. Jim braced himself as the storm broke over him. It was mostly about him having to clean up the mess even if it took him all day and how there were no servants in this house to go around after lazy thoughtless people, etc.

Jim had heard most of it before but it was heavy going just the same, especially as for once it wasn't his fault. When his mother ran out of steam she turned on her heel and stormed out.

She was right of course. Jim couldn't blame her, only this time she'd got the wrong person. He stood there with water dripping off his hair and his dressing gown sticking to his wet skin. Then he heard Pin laughing. He'd been hiding between the bath and the sink. Now he was rolling around the floor with tears of laughter running down his face. Unfortunately Mrs Doran heard the laughter too. She suddenly reappeared in the doorway.

'So you think it's funny?' she raged as she gripped Jim by the ear.

'No Mam, honestly...'

'Don't "honestly" me. I heard you sniggering,' she fumed as she marched Jim from the bathroom to his bedroom. 'Now you get yourself dried, tidy up that mess, scrub the bath and as an extra to cure your cheekiness, you can vacuum the hall, stairs and landing as well as your own room.'

'But Mam!' Jim protested.

'And if I hear another word out of you, you'll do Caitríona's room as well.'

Jim kept his mouth firmly shut. Having to clean Cat's room with her lying gloating on the bed, making sarcastic comments, was the stuff his nightmares were made of.

Mrs Doran left the room. Jim felt as if he'd been picked up by a whirlwind, tossed around for a few hours, then carelessly dumped. He heard a soft snigger. Pin had somehow followed them into the bedroom. He almost wished that Mam had accidentally stood on the little nuisance. He looked around but couldn't see him. Then he heard another smothered snort of laughter.

Jim got down on his knees and bending his head to the floor, looked under the bed. Pin dodged behind a pair of shoes but Jim saw the movement.

Just then Caitríona peeped in around the bedroom door. She had heard Mam giving out and was curious to know what it was all about. Oddly enough, though she frequently landed Jim in trouble by complaining about him, she usually felt sympathetic towards him whenever he landed himself in hot water. She was no stranger to the experience herself. Now she saw Jim on his knees. He obviously didn't know she was watching him.

'Come out here to me, you daft idiot!' he shouted at something under the bed.

'Jim, are you all right?' she asked. It sounded sarcastic though she didn't mean it to be.

'What?' said Jim, leaping up quickly with a look of guilty surprise on his flushed face.

'Who are you talking to?' asked Caitríona.

'Oh,' breathed Jim. 'It's my slippers. They won't come out.'

He was making fun of her again. 'Why don't you ask that little Pin-man to fetch them for you?' she replied angrily.

Then she turned on her heel and rushed out of the room in a rage.

As she slammed the door with more than her usual violence, she almost collided with her mother who was carrying clothes to the hotpress.

'For goodness sake, Caitríona!' exclaimed Mary Doran. 'There's no need to wreck the house.'

'But he's impossible,' complained Caitríona. 'He's in there talking to his slippers. I think you should call the doctor.'

'Just leave him alone,' advised her mother. 'He's probably over-excited about his birthday.'

'It's my birthday too,' said Caitríona, 'but I'm not going around acting like a lunatic.'

'Just be a little patient with him,' Mrs Doran urged. 'After all, he is your brother.'

Caitríona sighed dramatically and went off to her room.

Jim overheard their conversation and grinned to himself. That was just like Mam. Even when she was annoyed she'd still find an excuse for your behaviour.

He looked under the bed again but he could see nothing except shoes and dust. Obviously Pin wasn't going to come out and Jim couldn't get under the bed, so he left him there, dried his hair and got dressed. He couldn't clean the bathroom because Eileen had gone in and shut the door. He reckoned she'd be at least an hour doing herself up, so he hauled the vacuum cleaner into his bedroom and began his morning's tasks.

Jim found vacuuming really hard work and boring as well. Sometimes he would sing at the top of his voice to drown the sound and entertain himself — as well as annoy Cat. At other times he'd just let his mind wander.

He was in the middle of a day-dream about being able to make things move just by staring at them, when he felt a soft thud at the end of the vacuum. Then he heard a strangled squeak and was just in time to see Pin's feet vanishing into the nozzle. His golden buttons rattled all the way up the metal tubing. There was a violent hissing and a muffled whine from the engine as if it was blocked, then a sort of 'poomph!' and the suction sounded normal again.

Jim switched the vacuum off and kneeling close to it, he softly called, 'Are you all right?' There was no reply. 'Pin. Can you hear me?' he called more loudly. Still no reply. 'Don't panic. I'll get you out.'

Jim was just about to open the vacuum when he heard a noise behind him. He looked up. Cat was there again.

'I've heard it all now,' she declared. 'My little brother is talking to the vacuum cleaner.'

'You wouldn't hear anything if you weren't always spying on me,' Jim retorted. 'Anyway it's more fun talking to the vacuum than talking to you — it's more sympathetic.'

'And you're just a stupid — *boy!*' raged Cat. She spat out the final word as if it was a fearful insult. 'I'm not going to talk to you ever again.'

'Oh goody!' Jim cried as his sister vanished into her room.

He reached for the clips on the vacuum, wondering if Pin had broken his neck or even suffocated. Then he heard a delightful sound: 'Atishoo-yek!' — Pin's own personal sneeze.

He quickly got the top off the machine and released the dust-bag. There was a series of lung-shaking coughs and some rather indelicate curses. Then a ghastly-looking figure staggered out. He was covered from head to toe with grey dust, stray hairs, multi-coloured threads and bits of paper.

It was Jim's turn to laugh. Pin spat something filthy out of his mouth and was about to launch into a storm of abuse, when Jim caught him by the lapels of his jacket and lifted him up in front of his face.

'Now listen you,' Jim said, trying to sound threatening. 'You and I need to have a serious talk. You come into my house uninvited, you mess up my bathroom, you get me into trouble and then you laugh at me. If you're going to stay here you'll have to behave yourself. And what's more, I need to know who you are and where you came from and why you're here at all.'

Pin's face grew pale with shock beneath his coating of dirt. He looked so downcast that Jim began to feel sorry for him. 'Atishoo-yek!' he sneezed and a cloud of dust flew up from his head.

'You need a bath,' said Jim decisively. He set Pin down on the floor. 'Stay there,' he commanded. He put the vacuum together again. Then he looked round the bedroom door to check that the way was clear. He saw Eileen coming out of the bathroom with a towel wrapped around her head like a turban.

'Are you finished in there?' Jim asked.

'Yes.'

'Good. I've a job to do.'

'So I noticed,' replied Eileen.

Jim got a brown paper bag and went back to the bedroom. Pin was still sitting where he'd left him. He put the bag on the floor.

'Get in there,' Jim ordered.

'Why?' asked Pin, frowning.

'Because it's the safest way I can smuggle you into the bathroom. I'm not putting you into my pocket covered in all that filth.'

Pin got up grumbling darkly to himself and walked into the bag. Jim picked him up carefully and headed for the bathroom again. Once the door was locked he let Pin out.

Then he ran the bathwater, being careful not to make it too hot.

'Can you swim?' Jim asked.

'Like a fish,' boasted Pin.

'Show me,' said Jim.

Pin hopped up onto the rim of the bath and looked in. Then he shed his filthy clothes and without hesitating for a second he did a perfect dive into the water.

Jim really admired his courage and skill. While he loved swimming he had never learned to dive. It wasn't that he didn't know how, or that he hadn't tried, but somehow his courage always failed him at the last second. No amount of encouragement from his teacher or jeering from his friends could bring him to abandon himself to that scary plunge into space.

And now here was this tiny fellow diving into the bath. He sliced neatly through the water, came up with his hands by his side and shook his head.

'Lovely,' he gasped. Then he struck out and began doing lengths up and down the bath. It was the best crawl Jim had ever seen. Pin cut through the water making scarcely a wave or a bubble, while his feet flipped up and down like a paddling duck. When he reached the end of the bath below the taps, he flicked over and started off again. He did length after length like a real show-off.

There was a soap tray in the shape of a plastic duck beside the bath and a Mickey Mouse submarine that used to have a sponge stuck to the bottom of it. Jim dropped them into the water just to amuse — or annoy — Pin. Then he took the dirty clothes and rinsed them out in the sink.

Pin stopped showing off because Jim wasn't looking at him. He took a scrap of soap from the duck. Then he climbed onto the submarine and started soaping himself.

Jim squeezed out the clothes and hung them on the radiator to dry. Pin rinsed himself off by doing another few lengths underwater.

Meanwhile, with the help of a cloth and plenty of hot water, Jim began to clean up the toothpaste mess. It wasn't easy, especially with the bits of toilet roll in it and Jim began to feel grumpy again. When he looked in the bath, there was Pin sitting on the submarine resting his back against Mickey Mouse and paddling the craft along with his feet. He looked like someone on holiday in the Mediterranean. With a sudden rush of resentment, Jim snatched Pin and the submarine out of the water.

'Spoil-sport,' protested Pin.

'You've had enough sport for one day,' muttered Jim, setting the submarine down on the edge of the bath.

Pin wrapped himself in the corner of a towel and sat on the rim of the bath like a tiny king in an enormous cloak.

'Now,' Jim grunted, as he struggled on his hands and knees to clean the toothpaste out of the carpet, 'start explaining.'

Pin said nothing for a while. Jim looked up at him. He stared back solemnly, then he sighed heavily.

'The best I can do is explain why I can't explain,' he said.

'Don't talk in riddles,' Jim grumbled.

'It's the Great Law,' replied Pin heavily. 'If anyone tells about the rest of the Dominilli, they're never allowed to return.'

'You mean you'd be stuck here?'

'Yes.'

'And I'd be stuck with you.'

Pin didn't bother to reply to that.

'Who made this Great Law?' asked Jim.

'The Seniors,' Pin replied.

'So what's so dreadful about telling?' inquired Jim, feeling irritated that some group of high and mighty Seniors were preventing his curiosity being satisfied.

'It's part of the Wisdom of the Seniors from the Ancient Days,' replied Pin.

'The Ancient Days?' repeated Jim.

'Yes. From the time of the Great Disaster,' said Pin.

'What Great Disaster?'

Pin sighed again and looked reluctant to go on.

'Well?' persisted Jim. 'Don't stop now.'

'They called it the Years of the Giants,' replied Pin, with a note of real sadness in his voice. 'There. I've told you even more than I should.'

He began to rub his hair with the edge of the towel. It was clear he didn't want to say any more.

Jim was longing to know who these giants were and what kind of disaster they had caused in the Ancient Days. It sounded like a really interesting story. But he could see that Pin felt very deeply about it all and the Great Law was obviously a serious thing to him.

'All right,' he said. 'I won't ask you to break your Great Law, but I still need to know how you ended up in my bedroom.'

Pin looked sulky again.

'Well?' insisted Jim, sounding like his Dad demanding an explanation for one of his own stupidities.

'It was a sort of educational trip,' muttered Pin.

'Educational trip?' echoed Jim in disbelief.

'Yes,' said Pin. 'To learn about inventions and arrangements and try to understand the Big People.'

'I thought you wanted to avoid us,' said Jim.

'We do,' agreed Pin, 'but we need to know about you too. *Knowledge is a strong shield*, as the Seniors say.'

'So you were spying on us,' said Jim.

'Not spying really — more exploring.'

'How come you got left behind?'

'Ah,' he said, licking his lips and looking uncomfortable. 'That was a kind of accident.'

'Kind of?' said Jim sharply. 'You mean it was deliberate?'

'Oh, if you must know, I had a row with Strondilli, our Ducillo.'

'Ducillo?'

'Troop Leader, you would call him. He flew into a rage and stormed off. He didn't really mean it, but it was too late...' Pin's voice trailed off.

'Too late for what?' asked Jim.

'Too late to come back. Too late to bring me back with the rest.'

'Couldn't you find your own way back?' said Jim.

'It's not a matter of knowing the way so much as knowing how to make the crossing,' replied Pin. 'The Ducillo is the only one who has the, the — oh, the what-do-you-call-it!'

'What *do* you call it?' insisted Jim.

'We call it the formedat,' answered Pin. 'It means the gift-knowledge-ability.'

'What on earth does that mean?' exclaimed Jim.

'I don't know what word you people use for it,' replied Pin. 'I'm not very good at explaining things.'

'But you're pretty good at having rows with people,' Jim remarked drily. 'What'll happen when Strondilli arrives back without you?'

'He'll get into trouble. They'll send out a rescue party in case I'm being abused by a giant or being forced to tell on the rest of them.'

'Are you being abused?' asked Jim.

'No,' replied Pin. 'You're all right.'

'Well, thank you so much. It's nice to be appreciated,' said Jim, as he checked Pin's clothes and found to his surprise that they were already dry. 'Here. Get these clothes on. I've a lot of vacuuming to do, thanks to you.'

3   Nimble Fingers

When he got back to the bedroom, Jim put Pin on the bedside cabinet, beside his alarm clock.

'This isn't working,' remarked Pin, as he stood staring at the hands of the clock.

'I know,' sighed Jim. 'My Dad was supposed to try to fix it, but knowing him it'll be next year before he remembers.'

Vacuuming and talking don't mix, so Jim warned Pin to stay in the bedroom and keep out of sight while he got on with doing the bathroom floor and the landing. A few minutes later, when he returned to the room to unplug the flex, the back was off his alarm clock and all the cogs and wheels were spread out on top of the cabinet like a display of metal craftwork. Pin was standing in the middle of the chaos, leaning on a small screwdriver he had found in Jim's drawer. He had a look of idiotic satisfaction on his face.

'Oh no!' gasped Jim.

'Oh yes!' purred Pin. 'It's quite an ingenius invention.'

'What do you think you're doing?' shouted Jim.

'What does it look like?' Pin retorted, giving Jim a withering look. 'Go and finish your housework. The clock will be back together before you're finished.'

'It had better be,' Jim hissed through clenched teeth. He unplugged the flex and headed off to vacuum the stairs. He knew what would happen. That little disaster would wreck the clock completely, no doubt discovering that there were a few 'spare' cogs left over when he tried to put it together again. And Jim would be blamed for it, as usual. Pin was an unlimited trouble-maker. He swore that if Cat banged into his room and caught the little horror he wouldn't care.

Cat didn't bang into his room but she came walloping down the stairs and stood on the step where he was working.

'Good morning, vacuum cleaner,' she called to the machine. 'Have you spoken to any interesting lunatics recently?'

Jim swung the nozzle around, trying to suck her hair but the pipe was too long and he banged it off the stair-rails.

'Bye-ee, dust-sucker,' she called as she skipped down to the hall.

Jim muttered a few words that his Dad didn't like him to use and filled his mind with a daydream about what it would be like to live in a house where there were no sisters. Imagining that kind of heaven kept him happy right through the rest of the vacuuming. Then he dumped the machine outside Cat's room just to make sure she wouldn't forget to do her own work and went back to check on Pin.

He wasn't on the bedside cabinet but Jim's alarm clock was there, set at the correct time and ticking softly. There wasn't even a speck of dust left on the cabinet top. Jim looked around for the tiny clock-mender but there was no sign of him. Then he heard a soft contented sing-songing between his bed and the window. He listened carefully.

'Da bella goona danga,
Di vini musi dorn,
Do domro mino landa
Sa randa mina norn.'

There followed a soft humming of the same sweet-sad tune.

Quietly, so as not to disturb whatever was going on, Jim lowered himself onto the mattress and looked over the far edge.

Pin had found the huge box of Lego that Jim kept under his bed. He'd been collecting it for years, getting presents of it from aunts and uncles at Christmas and on his birthdays, so there was quite a lot of it. Pin was kneeling on the floor completely surrounded by the multi-coloured plastic bricks and all about him there rose the most amazing collection of buildings that Jim had ever seen. There were long halls with walls made almost entirely of doors; tall white towers with pointed tops; wide low buildings with roofs that were green on one side and red on the other; circular buildings all arches and courtyards; and structures that reminded Jim of sports stadiums.

Just then, Pin was putting the finishing touches to a village of beehive-shaped dwellings. It was fascinating to watch him. He was completely absorbed in his work, singing quietly to himself as his hands flicked across the scattered bricks, finding the ones he wanted and deftly slotting them into the complicated pattern he was weaving. The sharpness of his eye and the speed of his hands were incredible. Here indeed was a skilled craftsman in full flight.

Jim watched, hardly daring to breathe, as another beehive house took shape. Pin was placing each row of Lego bricks a little further in than the one below it and every row was a different colour from the last one. The doorway of the hut curved up to a point like a Gothic arch in an ancient monastery. Pin used clear plastic bricks for the top of the beehive to create the effect of a dome of glass that let light into the building. When it was complete, Pin sat back on his heels and gazed at it. Then he began to sing softly. It sounded almost like a love-song to the house he had made.

'La lenda sosa lorna,
Le norne sose lan,
In ente fore forno,
Di vini vori nan.'

It was a moment of quiet beauty and very private. As Jim gazed down at his new friend he began to think of Pin in a different way. It hadn't really occurred to him that Pin would have a language of his own. He had spoken English so well that Jim had taken it for granted. Now it seemed obvious that Pin had been speaking all the time in a foreign language. His real language was the one Jim had just heard him singing. Jim felt sure that the buildings Pin had made from Lego, really existed in his own country and that the song was the music of Pin's people.

Pin had lived a life full of experiences in a place that Jim really knew nothing about. He had been born of Dominillo parents and reared by them. He had made friends and dealt with enemies. He had been trained to do many skilful things and had set out on expeditions that were for him more dangerous than anything Jim had ever faced. He had a home that he obviously loved and friends that he no doubt missed. He had known all the complicated richness of a very long life.

Pin was gazing silently at his work. Then he sighed heavily and looked up.

Jim met his eyes without speaking and in that moment they both knew there was a new understanding between them.

'Pin, you're a genius,' said Jim.

'Only sometimes,' murmured Pin, with a regretful smile.

'What do you mean?' asked Jim. 'If you're a genius, you're a genius.'

'No one is a genius all the time,' replied Pin. 'I'm sure quite a lot of your scientific professors couldn't scramble an egg for themselves or iron a shirt. Are all your musical geniuses good at knitting pullovers?'

'I doubt it,' laughed Jim.

'And you've already discovered that I don't get everything right all the time!'

'You could say that all right,' agreed Jim. 'But tell me something else. How did you come to learn English so well?'

'Oh, we learn lots of languages,' answered Pin, with a careless shrug. *"Know the language: know the people."* That's an old saying among the Seniors. Wherever we go exploring, we listen carefully and learn how the people talk. Those who stay at home learn from the travellers.'

'You mean you can speak more languages?' said Jim in surprise.

'Of course,' replied Pin, pleased and amused that Jim was so impressed. 'Tá Gaeilge mhaith agam. Je parle bien Français. Jeg taler dansk. Ich spreche Deutsch. There's lots more, but I don't want to be too boastful.'

'Of course not,' murmured Jim. 'But how do you do it? We find learning languages very difficult. Most of my friends hate language classes.'

'That's because most of your people are Lodlumi,' said Pin.

'What's that?' asked Jim.

'The Lodlumi are a tribe who haven't bothered to train their memories,' replied Pin.

'Are they all stupid?' asked Jim.

'Not at all,' answered Pin. 'No more than you are. They

have an enormous amount of ability that they never use. We go to a lot of trouble to train our memories. All our children play memory games every day just for fun. We even have a sort of Memory Olympics, we call it the Musi-nan. The Seniors are all Musi-nani.'

'Musi-nani?'

'I suppose you would call them Olympic champions,' explained Pin.

'I wish I could improve my memory,' sighed Jim. 'My Mam says that some day I'll forget who I am.'

Pin looked up at him in surprise and suddenly burst out laughing.

'It's not really all that funny,' objected Jim.

'What's funny is that my mother used to say the very same thing to me when I was a little fellow,' replied Pin.

'If I could remember languages as well as you, I'd be considered a genius,' said Jim.

'Then become a genius,' declared Pin.

'How?'

'Train your memory.'

'How?' repeated Jim.

'Simple,' said Pin. 'Use it. Make it do things for you. Push it to the edges of its ability. Turn your head into a memory gymnasium and force it to exercise itself there every day.'

'Does it really work?' asked Jim.

'Of course,' replied Pin. 'If you were to train yourself to swim every single day wouldn't you expect to improve?'

'Sure,' agreed Jim.

'Well then,' continued Pin. 'If you exercise your memory every day, deliberately making it remember a little more every time, it will improve too and you'll be a genius!'

'I can't wait,' murmured Jim doubtfully. 'How do I start?'

'Shut your eyes,' commanded Pin.

Jim did as he was told.

'Now think of all the things that are on the cabinet beside your bed,' said Pin. 'Imagine them so that you can see them clearly in your mind, then without looking, tell me what you remember.'

'The bedside light,' began Jim. 'The clock that you fixed — and thanks for that — my school library book, a football card I got from the cereal packet yesterday... That's all, I think.'

'Not bad,' commented Pin. 'You forgot three things.'

From where he was sitting on the floor Pin could not see the bedside cabinet. Jim decided to test him out.

'All right,' he said. 'What did I miss — and no looking!'

Pin grinned up at him. 'You forgot the three drawing pins, two with red caps on them and one blue, the two silver-coloured coins and the bookmark with the scarecrow on it.'

Jim turned and looked. Pin was perfectly correct. 'Very good,' said Jim. 'You appear to know my room better than I do myself. Tell me more about this memory training.'

'When do you have to remember things, most often?' asked Pin.

'In school most of the time,' replied Jim, 'and whenever I'm sent on a message for Mam — though she often writes out a list of things.'

'Next time she gives you a list, look at it once, then go and get everything you can remember. Only when you think you're finished should you look at the list, just to make sure. You'll be surprised at how much you can remember. If you do that every time, you'll soon not need to use the list at all.'

Pin and Jim spent most of the morning playing memory games. Pin got him to try to learn off all the titles of the books on his bookshelves. Jim was surprised to discover that he had over fifty books in his own library. Then he had to recall the names of all the pupils in his class and where they were sitting. Jim showed Pin how to play chess and Pin proved his memory skill by remembering how every chess-piece moved after being told only once. Then they spent some time building with Lego. Pin was particularly interested in the spacecraft Jim made as he had never seen anything like that before. They were so preoccupied that Jim didn't notice the time passing until he heard his Dad calling him for lunch.

Jim decided against bringing Pin down to the kitchen. With the whole family seated around the table and Matsa patrolling the floor, the risk of his friend being discovered would be too great.

The Lego-and-memory session had left Jim in a warm contented humour. All through lunch he chatted good-humouredly with his family, ignoring Caitríona's attempts to provoke an argument. He even used his knife and fork properly and didn't speak with his mouth full of food. When the meal was over he surprised everyone by starting to clear the table without having to be asked. Caitríona decided that this was a further sign of his increasing mental disturbance.

'Whatever next?' she muttered as she rose from the table. 'If this new goody Jim is going to last all afternoon, I don't think I'll be able to stand the strain.'

'For goodness sake, Caitríona!' exclaimed Mr Doran. 'If Jim was annoying you, you'd be complaining. Why must you nag at him when he's being agreeable?'

Caitríona didn't reply to this rebuke but she shot Jim a black look as if her trouble was all his fault.

'You won't have to stand any strain,' put in Mrs Doran, anxious to avoid a row. 'You can come with me to the supermarket and help me with the shopping.'

Jim and Eileen cleared the table and washed up. Being a good deal older than Jim, Eileen wasn't very interested in her brother's doings and opinions. Jim found Eileen mildly boring.

Her life seemed to be made up of women's magazines, pictures of male pop stars and an incredible interest in clothes. But if they hadn't much to say to each other, they weren't rivals either and really didn't annoy each other very much. Besides, Eileen's lack of attention to him meant that Jim could get away with a lot more than he would have under Cat's ever-watchful eyes.

By the time Jim returned to Pin, his pocket contained half a grilled sausage that he had deliberately left on his plate, a slice of cheddar cheese that he had taken from the fridge when he was putting the milk away, a quarter of an apple that he had slipped into his pocket during lunch and a chocolate biscuit that he had expertly 'borrowed' while he was replacing the biscuit barrel on the worktop.

Pin was sitting behind a pile of school books on Jim's desk, trying to read a history text that he had set leaning up against the wall. The pages were almost as tall as himself.

'Lunch time!' Jim announced triumphantly as he set the feast on the desk.

'Oh goody!' exclaimed Pin. 'Food for the body as well as the mind.' He picked up the sausage and sniffed at it.'What is this?' he asked suspiciously.

'Sausage,' replied Jim. 'Have you never seen one before?'

Pin shook his head. 'What's it made of?'

'Pig meat, I think,' replied Jim. 'There's breadcrumb and spices in it as well.'

'Pigmeat!' exclaimed Pin with a look of disgust and he dropped the half-sausage as if it might wriggle alive and run grunting around the desk.

'Don't be such a silly,' protested Jim. 'It's perfectly safe and it tastes lovely. Besides I've gone to a deal of trouble to get it for you. I even did the wash-up with Eileen.'

'I'm sorry,' replied Pin. 'I don't want to appear ungrateful but we don't eat meat at all.'

'Why not?' asked Jim.

'Because to eat meat you have to kill animals,' replied Pin. 'Don't you think it's highly regrettable that we should slaughter other creatures and then eat their bodies?'

'I suppose it is,' murmured Jim doubtfully, 'but we have to eat and most animals kill and eat others — it's part of the way things are.'

'In my country there is plenty of food,' said Pin. 'No one needs to kill in order to eat. The creatures of the woods and fields live without fear.'

'We had a debate about this in school once,' said Jim, as he wrapped the offending sausage in a paper handkerchief and dropped it in his wastepaper basket. 'Our teacher said that if all the animals stopped killing each other the world would be completely overcrowded with creatures, including billions and billions of insects.'

'As your world is now, that is probably true,' admitted Pin, 'but it doesn't have to be that way. I believe that many of your creatures produce great numbers of young simply to ensure that at least some will survive the slaughter. If their young were not threatened by so many hungry enemies, their families would be smaller. At least that is the way it works with us. But speaking of hunger, I see you have some excellent cheese here and I have no difficulty in eating that, though I would appreciate a drink of water to wash down my feast.'

As Pin began to nibble at the slice of cheddar that was almost as long as his arm, Jim went down to the kitchen to get him a drink. At first he filled a mug from the tap. Then he realised that this would be like a barrelful to Pin, so he used a small eggcup instead. When he returned to his bedroom Pin was munching into the biscuit and his face was smeared with melted chocolate.

'What is this delicious brown stuff?' asked Pin, as he smacked his lips and tried to lick it off his chin.

'It's chocolate,' replied Jim. 'It's very popular here.'

'I can understand why,' mumbled Pin through another sweet mouthful. 'I could eat this stuff all day! Can you get me some more chocolate?'

'I'll have to be careful,' replied Jim. 'If I take too much they'll notice and I'll get into trouble. Anyway, you still have half a biscuit left. If you eat too much of it you'll be sick and it's not too good for your teeth either.'

'Nice things are always bad for you!' complained Pin.

'Here,' said Jim. 'Have a drink of water. That won't do you any harm, I think.'

Pin grinned at him, then he knelt down and drank from the eggcup. 'Not exactly spring water,' he said as he dabbed his mouth with a tiny handkerchief, 'but when you're thirsty you can't be fussy.' He sat down beside the quarter apple and began to nibble at the white flesh. 'Not bad,' he said. 'Somewhat lacking in flavour compared to the Rose-Glow Apples of Nanorda. At the end of autumn...'

'Jim!' Mr Doran's deep voice boomed up from the hallway.

'Trouble?' asked Pin, looking at Jim with raised eyebrows.

'I don't think so,' replied Jim. 'That's not his "Come-here-till-I-kill-you" voice. Just be ready to get out of sight.'

He went to the bedroom door. 'Here Dad!' he replied.

'I'm going to the hairdresser's,' said Mr Doran. 'You might as well come with me. You could do with a haircut to tidy you up for tomorrow.'

'All right,' answered Jim. 'I'll be down in a sec.'

'May I come?' asked Pin.

'Not unless you fancy spending an hour or more in my jacket pocket,' replied Jim.

'No thanks,' said Pin hastily. 'It'll be more entertaining here.'

'Just keep out of sight and out of trouble,' said Jim as he headed out the bedroom door.

'Of course,' answered Pin, with a naughty wink. 'What else would I do?'

'What else indeed?' muttered Jim uneasily, as he hurried downstairs to join his father.

4   A Mystery for Caitríona

In contrast with Jim's room, which was moderately tidy, and Eileen's room, which was a chaos of magazines and clothes, Caitríona's room was a perfect doll's house bedroom. Her pale pink wallpaper dotted with tiny blue flowers was set off perfectly by the deeper pink carpet. Sky-blue curtains framed her bright bay window that overlooked the Dorans' front garden. Her neatly made bed was covered with an unwrinkled white bedspread decorated with pink roses. Opposite the end of the bed stood a white dressing table with a large round mirror that Caitríona carefully polished every week. As Caitríona's mother was fond of repeating, her bedroom was a model for everyone else's.

Caitríona was very fond of pretty, colourful objects. Over the years she had turned her room into an Aladdin's Cave of knick-knacks bought out of her carefully-managed pocket money or given to her as presents by friends and relatives who knew what she liked.

Between her bed and the window there were two deep shelves filled with soft cuddly toys, including a smiling white teddy bear clutching a red rose, a green teddy with a shamrock on his white tummy, two pandas with their arms around each other's shoulders, a family of four penguins, a floppy pink flamingo, a grey and black dog that was really a hand puppet and a baby seal with sad appealing eyes.

The walls of her room were tastefully decorated with posters showing a stag gazing out from a snow-trimmed thicket, a polar bear licking her very cuddly cub and a friendly cat and dog rubbing noses.

Along the window Caitríona had hung a row of stained-glass mobiles, mostly of butterflies and birds, their soft blues, pinks and greens casting magic lights over her study desk that faced the window.

The deep shelf of the bay window was crowded with small glass and porcelain figures of animals, birds and people carrying flowers or baskets of fruit. There was also a glass bowl of clear marbles that captured the light and turned it into tiny curved rainbows.

On the dressing table there were two small baskets of dried petals and buds, known as pot-pourri. When she had first bought these they had filled her room with apple-orchard scents and she had driven everybody to distraction by endlessly talking about 'my pot-pourri'. Eventually Eileen found the phrase in her French dictionary and the next time poor Caitríona mentioned 'my pot-pourri', Eileen informed her and everyone else, that the words actually meant 'rotten pot'. After that Caitríona stopped trying to sound French and the scent gradually died away.

Between these faded glories Caitríona kept her two greatest treasures. One was a brass and copper music-box with a diamond-shaped mirror on the lid, framed by roses made from green and red glass beads. Whenever Caitríona lifted the lid to view the small store of jewellery she kept there, the box played 'The Last Rose of Summer' in tinkling fairy-land notes. Unfortunately the tune always stopped half-way through, ending with a few flat twangs. This was hardly surprising, as the box had belonged to her great-grandmother. It was too old now to repair, but Caitríona often wished she could hear it play the rest of the tune as it must have done the first time her ancestor had opened it long ago. Her other treasure was a hand-painted clockwork bird with a sharp little beak, two green glass eyes and shiny metal feet. Just below one of the bird's painted wings, a winding-up key was set into the metal bodywork. Caitríona's grandmother had given her the bird the Christmas before she died. When it was wound up, the bird took four unsteady steps, its beak pecked at invisible seeds, then it gave three squeaky cheeps and stopped. Sadly, the clockwork mechanism no longer worked and it was all Jim's fault.

One afternoon when Jim was nine years old and not at all as sensible as he now was, he wandered into Caitríona's room. He was feeling bored and wanted his sister to play with him. Caitríona wasn't there so Jim began to amuse himself with the wonderland of curiosities she had collected. It wasn't long before he realised that he was surrounded with marvellous chances for playing practical jokes on his sister. It was all so funny and exciting that he didn't think any further than the immediate delight of what he was doing.

He began by tying one of her shoes to the leg of the bed, using one end of the shoelace. The other end he tied to the next shoe and so on until he had all her well-knotted footwear in a captive line beside the bed. When Cat came in to change her shoes, she would have to pick up a pair of white and blue runners, her black ballet shoes, her best 'party' shoes, her

white gym shoes and an old pair of sandals that she should
have thrown out last year.

He found a leather-covered note-book in a drawer by her
bed. The first page announced in large capital letters, '*This is
Caitríona's strictly private diary. Strangers especially brothers,
keep out, by order.*'

He got great fun from reading her secret thoughts and
even greater enjoyment from changing her references to him.
'My horrible brother' became 'My lovely brother'. 'Stupid old
Jim' became 'Jim the genius'. He even wrote in the entry for
that night in advance. 'My friendly clever brother tidied up
my room today. What a surprise! It looks much more interesting now.' Jim finished it off with a scrawly drawing labelled 'Corny Cat!'.

Her night-dress was under her pillow. He put it on her
largest teddy, sat the bear up in the bed and gave it her private
diary to read. He lined up the rest of her soft toys in front of
the mirror, decorated them with her few pieces of jewellery
and sprayed them with a small bottle of perfume Caitríona
had never even used herself.

Then his eye fell on the painted bird. He wound it up and
it performed its short walk, pecked at the top of the dressing-
table and cheeped three times. Jim decided it would be good
fun to make it walk off the edge of the dressing table. He took
the bird in his hands and twisted the key forcefully. When it
was good and tight he gave it one more twist and heard a
sharp metallic crack! The bird trembled in his hand while its
works whirred briefly. Its metal feet struggled as if it was
trying to escape, then it cheeped once and was silent. Jim tried
turning the key again. It turned too freely. The springs didn't
tighten and when he released it, Cat's precious bird remained
dead. Only then did he realise that he had gone too far. He
fled from the room, half-hoping Caitríona wouldn't notice

the broken bird but knowing in his heart that she would.

There was an enormous row. Caitríona cried and screamed. Suddenly all the little jokes he had played weren't funny at all — they were acts of deliberate misbehaviour. Jim's mother shouted at him for ten minutes non-stop. He was sent to bed without any dinner and not allowed out to play for a week. He was strictly forbidden to enter Caitríona's room ever again, unless she invited him in.

For Jim this soon became a normal part of the rules of the house and he obeyed it without thinking. Unfortunately this did not apply to Pin. Jim had only been gone half-an-hour when Pin grew bored with the bedroom and decided to explore the house. He peeped around the door to make sure the coast was clear, then he tiptoed to the top of the stairs and listened carefully. The house was silent. He looked around, saw an open door and slipped quietly into Caitríona's room.

Jim and his father arrived back at the house almost at the same time as Caitríona and Mrs Doran. The children helped their mother to carry in the shopping and while Jim was bringing in the last bag of groceries Caitríona went upstairs.

Matsa was mewing at Jim's bedroom door. Caitríona wondered about this. Matsa wasn't allowed into the bedrooms and she usually didn't venture upstairs. Feeling sure that it was another sign that Jim was up to mischief, she shooed the cat downstairs and went into her own room.

The first thing she noticed was that the lid of her box of chocolates was open. She was certain that she had left it closed. Her best friend Laura O'Toole had given her the chocolates the previous day as a birthday present. Caitríona had opened the wrapping that evening and gazed upon the luxurious rows of smooth dark sweets, nestling in their paper cups. The delicious aroma of fresh chocolate made her mouth water. She had intended keeping the box intact until her actual birthday but changed her mind and allowed herself to eat just one of the chocolates — her favourite with a Brazil-nut in the centre. Now, as she looked inside, she saw three empty paper cups. She felt as if someone had hit her from behind and run away before she could see who they were. This was an insult and an outrage.

In a fine fury Caitríona stormed out of her room and burst into Jim's bedroom to confront the thief. There was no one there, though she was almost sure she heard a scampering noise as she entered. She glared around the room and her angry eye quickly found the evidence she wanted. Beside Jim's alarm clock there was a half-eaten chocolate caramel. She was about to turn to the door when she noticed something else. The alarm clock showed the correct time. The second hand was moving steadily around the clock-face and she could hear a soft ticking.

The door creaked behind her and turning she saw Jim standing there with a look of surprise on his face.

'What are you doing in my room?' he demanded.

'What were you doing in mine?' she countered.

'Don't be silly,' Jim replied. 'I never go into your room.'

'Really?' retorted Caitríona, raising her eyebrows sarcastically. 'What about this then?' And she pointed accusingly at the bedside cabinet.

The half-chocolate was gone. Caitríona's finger was pointing at a small brown smear on the white cabinet top.

'Listen Cat,' said Jim quietly, 'I'm not being deliberately stupid, but am I supposed to see something?'

Caitríona stood with her finger still pointing, a look of astonishment on her face and her mouth open.

Jim looked at her uneasily. 'Nice try Cat,' he said. 'You almost had me fooled.'

'But it was there a few seconds ago!' she croaked, as she found her voice again.

'What was?' asked Jim.

'One of my chocolates,' she replied, her face beginning to flush with anger and embarrassment. 'It was half-eaten.'

'I didn't know you had chocolates,' said Jim. 'Were you keeping them for yourself?'

'Somebody stole them,' insisted Caitríona, glaring angrily at her brother.

Jim thought uneasily of Pin and the chocolate biscuit. 'I'm not the thief,' he said. 'Anyway, if I stole a chocolate I'd eat it. I wouldn't leave half of it beside my bed. I'm not that stupid.'

'Humph!' said Caitríona and managed to make it sound as if she thought Jim's lack of intelligence was beyond measuring.

'I'm going to tell Mam, so I am,' she declared and she strode angrily from the room.

Jim groaned. He would be blamed, of course. Who else could they possibly accuse? 'Pin!' he growled. 'Where are you, you bloomin' idiot?'

At the top of the stairs Caitríona heard him mumbling. She hesitated for a moment, then she came back and stuck her head around Jim's door.

He turned on her with a face like thunder. 'What do you want now?' he snapped.

She glanced suspiciously around his room, then looked at him accusingly. 'How come your alarm clock is working again?' she asked.

The question took him by surprise. He stared at the clock as if he hadn't seen it before. 'Working?' he echoed.

'Yes, numbskull,' she replied. 'Working. Or hadn't you noticed?'

'Oh yes,' he admitted. 'Yes. It's going again.'

'Did Dad fix it?' she asked, knowing full well that he hadn't. Whenever her father succeeded in fixing anything, he announced it proudly to the whole household to make sure they appreciated how clever he was.

'Er, no,' replied Jim thinking frantically. 'It fell off the cabinet while I was dusting and when I picked it up it was ticking again. Peculiar isn't it?'

'Very peculiar,' agreed Cat. 'Just like my half-eaten chocolate.'

As she slammed Jim's door behind her, Caitríona was already rehearsing the complaint she would make to her mother. Then her quick mind thought of something else and she headed back into her own room. She had a feeling that more than the chocolates had been interfered with. She looked carefully around. Everything seemed to be in order. She inspected the chocolate box again in case any more sweets had mysteriously vanished, but the box was just as she had left it.

She sat down on the edge of her bed, wondering if she was becoming too suspicious. Then her eye landed on the jigsaw puzzle laid out on her desk by the window and she gasped in surprise. It was a three-thousand-piece picture of Bunratty Castle and Folk-Park. Caitríona had been working on it for almost two weeks and it had been proving rather difficult. In fact she had abandoned the unfinished puzzle in a mood of frustration several days ago. Now it was perfectly finished!

Caitríona stood up and slowly eyed every object in her room. All her books and pens were exactly as she had left them but there was something not quite right. Then she saw it. The rubic cube that she had left unsolved long ago now showed sides of pure colour — yellow, red, blue, green, white and orange.

Who could have done all this? Surely Jim wouldn't have had either the time or the ability to complete an awkward jigsaw full of pieces showing green leaves and grey rocks that might fit in almost anywhere. As for the rubic cube, he had once given it a few twists, then thrown it aside saying it was 'stupid'. She remembered saying, 'You're the one that's stupid!' as she took it, intending to solve it and show it off to him. She had never succeeded.

Now she had a real mystery to solve. Her parents wouldn't do such a thing and Eileen hadn't the slightest interest in either jigsaws or rubic cubes. That only left Jim and he couldn't have ...

An uneasy shiver trickled down Caitríona's spine. She moved carefully around her room, examining everything minutely, searching for some other piece of evidence that might explain everything. All her ornaments were in their proper places. The soft toys looked as cute and cuddly as they always did.

She stood in front of the mirror and stared at herself, half-expecting to see some sort of clever ghost leering over her shoulder. Then, as if to comfort herself, she picked up her precious painted bird and looked fondly at its reflection in the mirror. Without thinking she turned the winding key. Instantly the works whirred beneath her fingers.

Caitríona was so startled that she leaped back, dropping the bird onto the dressing table. It fell on its side and began to spin helplessly in circles until the key stopped turning.

It was a full minute before Caitríona had the courage to pick the bird up again. When she did, she turned the key three times, noticing how firmly it wound. She set the bird carefully on its legs and released it. It walked stiffly across the dressing table, its metal feet slipping slightly on the smooth surface. Then its head bobbed up and down as it pecked for food while it gave five cheerful cheeps. Finally, it flipped over onto its back and waved its shiny legs in the air!

Caitríona wasn't so sure she liked the gymnastics, but there could be no doubt about the fact that her bird wasn't just fixed — it was very much improved! The mystery was growing even more puzzling: no one in the house could have repaired that bird.

The music box was near her hand. She touched it wondering, half-hoping, half-afraid. Then she took a deep breath and opened the lid. As the tune of 'The Last Rose of Summer' tinkled clearly, Caitríona could see that her jewellery had been disturbed. It had been put back carefully and neatly but it wasn't in the same order as she had left it. She waited for the tune to break down at its usual place. It didn't stop. It kept on playing. Not only that but the melody began to speed up. Faster and faster it played as if the tune was a ridiculous musical race, until the lid suddenly snapped shut, making her jump in surprise. Obviously her mystery handiman didn't always get things right.

What was she going to do now? Of course she could rush downstairs and tell her parents everything. They wouldn't believe her at first but the evidence was there and they'd be astonished by what she could show them. It would cause quite a disturbance in the house. There'd be a lot of talk and Jim would be closely questioned or maybe given out to. Even if he was responsible, he would deny everything — he always did. But Caitríona guessed that once the excitement had died down, nothing further would be done about it. She'd be no closer to solving the mystery and that, more than anything else, was what she wanted to do.

She decided to remain silent and think and wait ...

5   Happy Birthdays?

One of the disadvantages of being twins was that Jim and Caitríona rarely had birthday parties with their friends.

Sometimes, when they were younger, they each had their own party on different days. But on her eighth birthday, two of Caitríona's friends had over-eaten and had been sick on the sitting-room carpet. At Jim's party his pals had raced up and down the stairs like a herd of mentally-disturbed buffalo, until one of them tripped and crashed through the glass in the front porch. After that, Mr and Mrs Doran had vowed that they'd never go through it all again. Since then the double birthday had become a family celebration that included visits to aunts and uncles. On these occasions, everyone pretended to be surprised by the production of colourfully wrapped birthday presents and the children's mother always exclaimed, 'Oh, you shouldn't have bothered!' Jim and Caitríona often wondered what she'd say if they actually didn't bother, but they had to agree that it was a great way of gathering gifts.

That Sunday morning Jim and Caitríona found their presents in their places at the breakfast table as usual. Caitríona got the instamatic camera she'd been hoping for, the kind that produces the developed photo a few minutes after you take the shot. Jim was delighted to get a Walkman and a tape of all the number one hits of the past year.

While he was giving his Mam a thank-you kiss, Caitríona took a flash photo of them and threatened to show it to all the girls in school. Jim chased her round the table trying to snatch the photo and a row was only avoided by Eileen arriving down with her presents for the two of them. She gave Caitríona a little necklace of blue beads in a blue velvet box with a blue silky lining. To Jim she gave an Airfix kit of a Harrier GR-5, the kind that has all the tiny parts of the aeroplane set in plastic frames and complicated instructions with mysterious diagrams.

Jim was pleased with his present and thanked Eileen, but Caitríona couldn't let the matter go by without having her say.

'I hope you make a better job of it than you did with the last one,' she remarked scornfully.

The last plane was a Hawker Siddeley Buccaneer S.2B that Jim had bought for himself, after seeing some models hanging from the ceiling of a schoolfriend's bedroom. He'd been too impatient to study the diagrams or read the instructions and had rushed ahead presuming it would be obvious where everything would go. It wasn't. At the end he found he had several pieces left over with nowhere to put them, so he decided they were 'spares'. The 'finished' plane was all gaps and cracks and blobs of glue. When the glue was well set, Jim discovered he'd put on the tail wings back to front and there were bombs where the landing wheels should have been.

His father found it mildly amusing. 'I think you've invented a new type of warplane,' he said. 'Probably intended to bewilder the enemy!'

Caitríona had teased him for months about it so that he hadn't the courage to buy another one and try again. Now Eileen's gift was exactly what he needed and he resolved to take his time and get it right, even if it took him to Christmas to finish it.

Then Jim and Caitríona exchanged presents. Caitríona gave him 'The Book of a Hundred Jokes'. On the fly-leaf she had written: 'To Jim from Caitríona. Happy birthday. Hope this improves your humour!'

Jim liked the present but not the comment. However, as this was the usual nature of their exchanged presents, he was ready with his own dart of wit.

When Caitríona unwrapped the pretty wrapping paper from the little parcel Jim gave her, she found a lovely hand-mirror framed with lozenges of coloured glass. It was exactly the sort of thing she liked and for a second she felt grateful to her brother for knowing her so well. A small card was taped to the back of the mirror and on it Jim had written his birthday message: 'To Cat. Now you'll be able to see what the rest of us have to look at. Have a happy birthday — if possible! Your patient brother, Jim.'

'You really know how to spoil things, don't you?' she said.

'Yes,' he replied. 'I learnt it from you.'

'Having your usual birthday battle?' said Mr Doran as he breezed into the kitchen. For reasons that none of his children could understand, their father was always in good humour on their birthday. 'Now,' he declared, 'I am going to have a large, happy, relaxed, peaceful breakfast — and so are you!' He smiled broadly as he said it and Jim was reminded of the face of a Mexican bandit, who smiled sweetly while robbing the stagecoach at gunpoint.

They all had a peaceful breakfast!

Afterwards Jim brought his cards and presents upstairs to show them to Pin. He was quite curious about the plane — the idea of a large machine flying through the air seemed astonishing to him — but he showed little interest in anything else and Jim thought he was looking rather glum. However he did cheer up when Jim produced a large juicy plum from his pocket.

'You are becoming quite a useful thief,' Pin remarked as he set the fruit between his knees and bit into its sweet ripe flesh.

While Pin was eating, Jim searched in his new joke book for something to cheer his friend up.

'Hey Pin,' he said. 'Listen to this. Why couldn't the elephant make a phone-call to the zoo?'

Pin looked at him blankly. 'Tell me,' he said.

'Because the lion was engaged!' giggled Jim.

Pin looked puzzled. 'Who was he marrying?' he asked.

'He wasn't marrying anyone,' sighed Jim. 'I was using the word *lion* in place of the word *line*. It's called a pun and it's meant to be funny.'

'That's a funny way to be funny,' remarked Pin, drily.

'How about this one?' persisted Jim. 'A policeman saw a man with a briefcase running down the street. Thinking he looked suspicious, he stopped him and said, "I suppose you are training for a race?" "No," replied the man. "I'm racing for a train!" and he dashed into the station.'

'Ha!' cried Pin. 'Another play on words. Very punny!'

'Oh no!' groaned Jim. 'You're worse than the book.'

'You started it,' said Pin with a devilish smirk on his face, 'so you'll have to take your *pun*ishment!'

'Argh!' growled Jim as he shut the joke book. 'All right, no more jokes.'

Just then there was a loud knock on the bedroom door. Pin dropped to the floor and vanished under the bed. The door opened and Jim's Dad stuck his head in.

'We're going to the Club,' he said. 'Are you ready?'

'I'll be down in a minute,' replied Jim.

As soon as the door was closed Pin crawled out again.

'Where are you going?' he asked.

'It's the Kilternan Country Club,' replied Jim. 'They have a swimming pool and a gym and a games room and a golf course and lots of other things.'

'Sounds like my kind of place,' said Pin and his face brightened with interest. 'May I come too?'

'Hmmm,' said Jim. 'I'm not so sure that would be a good idea.'

'Why not?' insisted Pin.

'How would you fancy sharing a swimming pool with twenty giants all splashing and thrashing around?' Jim asked.

'Not a lot,' admitted Pin. 'Isn't there anything I could do up there?'

'I could bring you along in my sports bag with the towels and things,' said Jim, 'but you'd have to stay in the dressing-room while I was swimming. In fact you'd really have to stay in the bag. The dressing-rooms are usually pretty busy and if anyone saw you even peeping out you'd have no chance of escaping. I think you'd be better off staying here.'

Pin looked glum again. 'Oh well,' he sighed. 'You go and enjoy yourself. Don't worry about me.'

'Jim!' called Mr Doran's voice from the bottom of the stairs. 'We're going now.'

'Coming Dad!' shouted Jim. He looked at Pin's sulky face. 'Listen Pin,' he said. 'I've no choice. I have to go. You're a lot safer here and I'll be back before lunch. Now, don't do anything silly while I'm gone. See you later. OK?'

It was obvious from Pin's face that it wasn't OK, but Jim couldn't wait to argue further, so with a final 'Bye!' he left the room, feeling a bit irritated with his friend for making him feel guilty.

The Dorans had a family membership at the Country Club and they all travelled to Kilternan that morning as part of the birthday celebration. While Tom and Mary Doran worked out in the gym, the children played table-tennis and snooker. Then everyone went for a swim in the pool.

Jim had such a good time that he forgot about Pin's sulky humour until they were leaving the club. Then his father anounced that they wouldn't be going home, as their Aunt Therese and Uncle David had invited them to lunch. Jim felt a stab of regret for Pin. He could imagine the complaints he would have to face for not returning when he said he would, but there was nothing he could do about the situation. He was really looking forward to playing with his cousin Christopher, who had lots of computer games, so he decided to enjoy his birthday treat and worry about Pin later.

As it happened, the Dorans spent the whole day out. After their lunch they went to the children's Aunt P. Her real name was Pádraigín but the children had been unable to manage this when they were toddlers, so they had named her P and the handy label had stuck so well that even the adults used it now. Aunt P had a dog called Rocky who played a nifty game of football and kept Jim and Caitríona entertained for an hour and a half in the back garden while the adults and Eileen chatted inside.

After that they all went down town for a game of bowling followed by dinner in the Jasmine House Chinese restaurant.

Meanwhile Pin was at home on his own. Long before

lunchtime he grew bored and to pass the time he began to examine Jim's presents again. The print in the joke book was too large to read close up but he found that if he propped it up on a pillow and stood well back, he could read it comfortably. He had a good giggle at some of the jokes, but many of them were just silly and he couldn't understand a lot of the others. He tried to work the Walkman but the tape was too awkward for him to insert.

Then he opened the aeroplane kit. Before long he was on his knees on Jim's desk with the plans and instructions spread out beneath him. As his nimble fingers began to detach the parts of the plane from their plastic frame he started to hum contentedly to himself. By the time he was squeezing out the glue, he was singing. It was almost lunchtime before he sat back on his ankles to admire his finished work. He had assembled a perfect model of a Harrier GR-5.

Pin stood up and stretched. He listened for the sound of the family returning but the house was totally silent. He was feeling self-satisfied and confident and also rather hungry.

'Well,' he said to himself, 'I'm supposed to be on a fact-finding mission. So let's find some facts — and maybe some food!'

He leaped from the desk to the bed and climbed down the sheet to the floor. Then, with his screwdriver tucked under his arm like a lance, he set off exploring.

Pin crept cautiously from the bedroom and slid silently down the stairs on his bottom, keeping a watchful eye out for Matsa. As luck would have it, Matsa had been let out before the Dorans left for the club and she was happily scent-marking a neighbour's garden and digging holes in the flower-bed.

Pin advanced down the hallway and through the open kitchen door until he found himself standing on a vast expanse of red lino, squared-off to look like floor-tiles. Giant white chairs and a huge round table loomed above him. A towering white fridge hummed to itself beside a row of pinewood cupboards.

The kitchen was full of food-smells: a hint of scrambled eggs lingered near the cooker; a trace of toast hung around the worktop, blending with a sweetness of fruit from a basket of oranges, grapes and plums. Pin began to feel an urgent need for food and the memory of chocolate biscuits awoke in his mind. He tried to pull open one of the pinewood doors but it was too solid to be moved from the bottom by someone as small as him.

He looked carefully around. There was obviously a deep worktop on top of the cupboards and there were some interesting looking containers up there. A clothes-horse stood in front of a radiator at the far end of the room.

'Almost as good as a ladder,' Pin murmured to himself as he skipped across the floor. He left the screwdriver on the lino, then with a light jump, he caught hold of the first rung of the clothes-horse. Then he pulled himself up, got his feet on the rung and sprang at the next one. His gymnastic training at the Bendovina Woods had left him as agile as a monkey and within a few seconds he was level with the worktop. One last courageous leap, and he landed on the shiny surface beside a very inviting row of kitchen containers.

His next problem was to find out what was inside them. He tried sniffing at them but the various scents blended with each other, though he was sure there was chocolate nearby. He found that he could reach the rim of the lid by stretching his arms fully above his head. A little push would surely do the trick. He jumped, striking the container with his fists. The lid flew off, but the force of the blow knocked the container over and it crashed onto its side spilling out a mound of white crystals, like an avalanche of shattered ice.

'Oops!' exclaimed Pin. 'Another little mess.'

He picked up a handful of the crystals and put one of them in his mouth. It was very sweet — too sweet indeed for him to want to eat any more of them. He tried to tidy up the mess by throwing handfuls of the stuff back into the fallen container but it was a tiresome task. Then he tried using the lid as a shovel. That worked better but he found he couldn't push the container upright again. As he was setting the lid down he noticed a label stuck to the top saying, 'Sugar'.

'Of course,' he said to himself. 'I've read about that stuff. *A general sweetener much loved by human children. Very bad for your teeth.* I wonder if the rest of these boxes are labelled? It would save me a deal of trouble and avoid a few messes!'

By standing on the sugar-lid he found he could reach the top of the next container with his hands. One good heave and he was on the top. Sure enough there was another label beneath his feet. This one said, 'Flour'. Pin was glad he hadn't tried to open that one. He stepped onto the next container. 'Biscuit Barrel' was written on the top.

'Now we're in business!' he chuckled, licking his lips. As it was impossible to open the lid while he was standing on it, Pin climbed down again. He tried his leap-and-punch trick but it didn't work this time. The lid was too firmly pressed down. He tried again, using all his strength. The barrel toppled over on its side, rolled across the worktop and fell with a crash to the floor. Pin peeped carefully over the edge. The barrel was lying near the table. It was still in one piece but the lid had shot off and rolled across the floor and some of the biscuits had fallen out.

Pin climbed back down. Then he took a red and white table-napkin from the clothes-horse and spread it on the floor. In the mouth of the barrel he found a large, unbroken biscuit covered in dark chocolate. He placed this carefully on his napkin. The rest he replaced in the barrel. Then he moved the barrel against a leg of the table and managed to push the lid on again.

He felt a little tired after all this work, so he sat on his napkin and bit a mouthful from the biscuit. It was delicious. While he sat happily munching, he considered his situation. There was a mess of sugar on the worktop and a container on its side. The floor around him was covered with biscuit crumbs and he knew there was no way he could put the biscuit barrel back in its proper place. When Jim's family got back there was going to be trouble.

He bit into the biscuit again. What was it the Seniors always said? When you can't undo the harm you've done, make up for it by doing something good. What could he do? He looked about him. Then he saw the toaster. Jim had said that it didn't work properly. Perhaps he could fix it.

He took another bite from the chocolate biscuit, then broke off a piece and put it in his pocket to keep him going while he was working. Taking careful aim, he threw the screwdriver up onto the worktop, then he climbed up the clotheshorse again. Before long he was unscrewing the side of the toaster, carefully placing the small screws in a neat row so that he would remember where they went when he was putting things back together again. It took him quite a while to figure it out, but once he'd located the problem, he set to work loosening, adjusting, reconnecting and finally replacing everything just as he'd found it. He didn't want to add any further disasters to his list of 'accidents'. Unfortunately he couldn't check to see if his improvements worked because the toaster had been unplugged and the socket was too high on the wall for him to reach.

While he was on the worktop, Pin helped himself to a grape from the fruit basket, then he returned to the floor.

Things were going rather nicely for him so he decided to explore further. Towing his biscuit along behind him in the napkin, he headed for a large varnished door that wasn't quite closed.

The gap was just big enough to allow him to squeeze through, though he had to pull the napkin with the biscuit very carefully after him. He was in a long room with a very large window at the far end. As he walked across the floor Pin sank to his ankles in the deep pile of the carpet. It was like crossing a field of brown and gold grass. In front of the window there was a television set and in the corner between the window and the fireplace, a piano with a wind-up piano stool.

Pin was excited by the wide open space and the soft floor-covering. Abandoning his napkin, he performed a ballet of bodily delight, dashing across the floor and leaping into the air like an olympic gymnast, turning cartwheels, doing somersaults and always landing neatly and firmly on his feet. He ended up at the window, panting and glowing from the exercise.

'Now for a little climbing,' he muttered.

He gripped the long curtains in his hands and hoisted himself off the floor, then using his arms and legs he worked his way up, moving like a caterpillar along a leaf.

Soon he was level with the keyboard of the piano. The rows of black and white keys looked interesting so he jumped onto them. The jarring noise of the notes as his feet hit the keys startled him so much that he fell over and made an even worse sound. He lay quite still until the vibrating notes faded, then he stood up carefully. Immediately a white key sank beneath his feet, playing a single sweet ringing note. He stepped onto the next key, and a slightly lower note sounded. Leaning over he pressed a black key with both his hands and was rewarded with a rich tone like a bell.

Pin smiled to himself. 'Of course,' he breathed. 'It's a musical instrument — a bit like our coridano.'

He walked carefully along the keys playing a descending scale until he reached the centre of the piano. Then he decided to have some fun. He began to dance along the keyboard, now on the white keys, now on the black, leaping into the air and landing on two feet, hopping along playing with one foot, standing on his hands and playing up and down the scales while his legs waved in the air. All the while he sang or shouted 'Ah-loo!' which was his word for 'Yippee!'

In a moment of overpowering enthusiasm, he did a continuous cartwheel from the top of the keyboard to the middle, where he sprang into the air gripping his knees, spun head over heels and sailed right off the piano. Fortunately he landed smack on the piano-stool, where the force of his landing made the circular seat spin around twice. He laughed like a child on a merry-go-round and by pushing with his hands against the piano he found he was able to keep the stool-seat spinning until it had wound down completely.

The sudden halt to his ride flung him from the stool and he shot through the air, narrowly missing the stone hearth and landing on a thick sheep-skin rug. Here he lay, gasping for breath.

'That was a close one,' he panted to himself. 'Mustn't get too carried away.'

When he had recovered, he returned to his biscuit and strengthened himself with another mouthful of chocolate. Then he climbed up onto the couch. This was a soft, bouncy place. He tried a few leaps up and down as if he was on a trampoline but he soon unbalanced and fell backwards onto something hard that had been left on one of the cushions.

To Pin's terror the room was suddenly filled with banging,

clanging and wailing. The dark box over by the window lit up to reveal four weirdly dressed men with purple and green hair, who writhed about with expressions of agony on their faces while they struggled violently with what looked like musical instruments.

The terrified Pin held his hands up to his ears and staggered backwards. His foot pressed a button on the hard black object and suddenly the four demons disappeared and in their place he saw a wide green field over which men in peculiar uniforms were running.

'This is surely some form of magic!' exclaimed Pin to himself, wondering how a field could appear inside a house.

All the men wore short trousers and each of them had a number on his back. As Pin watched he realised there were two groups, one with red tops to their uniform and the other with blue. At first he thought they might be armies on the field of battle but instead of attacking each other they raced around trying to gain possession of a small round object that bounced along the grass. The odd thing was that as soon as one of them got the round thing, he walloped it away from himself again.

The shock of all these apparitions made Pin feel weak. He sat down and instantly the scene changed again. Now he could see a kind-looking woman breaking eggs into a bowl and whisking them up while she advised him to have his flour already sifted before he began to make his Christmas cake.

Pin stared at her in wonder as she continued to talk while she added flour and fruit to her bowl.

Then he looked at the object he was sitting on. It was covered with buttons. Many of them had numbers on them, others showed strange signs like arrowheads or circles with colours in them, or plus or minus signs. Pin stood up and pressed his foot against number three. Straight away the woman disappeared and in her place he saw a family seated around a table. Their shining faces beamed with amazing delight as their mother set a steaming bowlful of peas in front of them. Pin had never seen anyone look so happy about eating peas.

'Maybe peas are very scarce here,' he muttered and he decided to ask Jim about it later.

He pressed number five and was horrified to see a girl's terrified face. Next moment he saw the cause of her fear. A man with a look of sheer evil on his face and madness burning in his eyes, was chasing the girl down a dark stairway and in his upraised hand he held a savage knife.

'Stop!' cried Pin stepping forward.

The screen went blank. Pin froze as he was, not daring to move. After a while he looked down and saw that his foot was on a red button. There was a green button next to it. He stood on that one. The screen lit up again. This time he saw top class gymnasts performing in front of a cheering crowd of people.

'Ah, Bendovinani!' cried Pin, delighted to see something he could understand.

After a little more experimenting, he discovered how to reduce the volume, change the brightness and so on. Once he realised he was in control of the 'apparitions' he felt less afraid. When the gymnastics were over he found a group of musicians playing Irish dance music and he pranced about in time with the reels, jigs and hornpipes.

He felt tired then and a bit peckish, so he raided the kitchen again for more fruit and biscuits. He towed these in on his napkin and settled down contentedly to watch a programme of cartoons. He particularly enjoyed Bugs Bunny.

It was only when the headlights of the Dorans' car flashed

into the driveway that Pin realised he'd been watching television all afternoon and that he was sitting in the half-darkness. He heard the car doors slam and the voices of the family getting out and panic seized him. He pushed half-a-dozen grapes and a chocolate biscuit down behind the cushions, leaped onto the remote-control to switch the television off and accidentally increased the volume. Frantically he stabbed at the red button and as the television died, Pin was sprinting out of the room and through the kitchen. When Mr Doran inserted his key in the front door, Pin was half-way up the stairs and by the time the hall light was turned on, he was safely back in Jim's bedroom.

6   Puzzles for Everyone

'That's peculiar,' said Tom Doran. 'I could have sworn I heard the television.'

'I heard it too,' agreed Eileen.

'Maybe it was next door's you heard,' suggested Jim. 'Ours is obviously off.' He had his own suspicions though and while the others stood in the hall taking off their coats, he slipped into the sittingroom and turned on the light. The television was definitely off. Jim walked over and put his hand on the back of the set. It was warm.

'The little monkey!' he whispered to himself. He looked carefully around the room but there was no sign of Pin. Then he heard voices raised in the kitchen. He went to see what the fuss was about and immediately found himself accused of misbehaviour.

'Are you responsible for this?' demanded his mother.

'For what?' asked Jim trying to sound as innocent as he truthfully was.

'This mess on the worktop,' replied Mary Doran, 'and that mess on the floor.'

Jim looked and saw the upset sugar container and a scattering of crumbs around the fallen biscuit barrel.

'How could I have anything to do with that?' he asked. 'I was out all day with everyone else.'

This was obviously true and it also meant that no other member of the family could be accused either. Mrs Doran grunted in frustration and picked up the biscuit barrel. As she took it in her hand the lid fell off to reveal that their store of biscuits had strangely decreased since morning.

'Now here's a nice mystery,' she muttered. 'Someone upsets the sugar and doesn't bother to tidy it up. Then they steal biscuits — mostly the chocolate ones — and leave the barrel lying on the floor.'

'Could it have been Matsa?' asked Eileen.

'She's been out all day too,' replied Caitríona and she gave Jim a look that said "I know more than you think I do", though what she was pretending to know she wasn't even sure herself.

'We've hardly been burgled?' murmured Tom Doran.

Everyone looked at him in alarm.

'There's no sign of any disturbance in the sittingroom,' said Jim, who had his own ideas about the 'burglar'.

'I'd best check upstairs,' said Tom Doran doubtfully and Caitríona hurried after him to make sure her room hadn't been interfered with again. Meanwhile Mrs Doran went into the sittingroom to satisfy herself that what Jim said was true. Thinking that Pin might still be in there, Jim followed her.

'What's this napkin doing in here?' asked Mrs Doran.

Jim didn't feel he was expected to answer, so he remained silent.

When his mother bent down to pick up the napkin, she

noticed a grape wedged between the cushions on the couch. She lifted the cushion and discovered the rest of the grapes and the chocolate biscuit.

As soon as Jim saw the biscuit he turned and headed for the door but just then Caitríona came into the room, followed by Eileen who wanted to see her favourite television programme. Tom Doran was right behind them.

'Everything's all right upstairs,' announced Mr Doran. 'By the way Jim, you made a great job of that aeroplane. How on earth did you manage to get it done so quickly?'

Jim stared at him in confusion.

'Have you finished it already?' gasped Eileen.

'I don't...' began Jim. Then he stopped. He'd been about to say, 'I don't know what you're talking about,' when the truth dawned on him. He stood open-mouthed for a second, then his mother saved him from having to explain.

'Take a look at this,' she commanded, pointing dramatically at the couch. By the edge in her voice Jim knew there was going to be more trouble.

Everyone looked at the remains of Pin's snack.

'All right,' breathed Tom Doran as he faced his three children. 'Who is responsible for this? It has to be one of you three.'

Of course no one admitted doing it and their parents couldn't figure out when or how the mischief had been done. Everyone felt exasperated.

'I think the best thing for you all to do, is to go to your rooms and leave your mother and I in peace for a few hours,' decided Mr Doran.

It was an unsatisfactory end to an otherwise enjoyable day and both children and parents felt unhappy about it. As Jim headed up the stairs he resolved that Pin was going to pay for his mischief.

The bedroom was in darkness as Jim entered. He switched on the light and closed the door behind him. There was no sign of Pin. 'No wonder he's hiding,' he muttered to himself. He was just about to issue a red hot series of blood-chilling threats to the room in general, when he had a crafty idea. It occurred to him that Pin might be unaware that his misbehaviour had been discovered and he would be more likely to come out if he thought that Jim was in good humour. Once he was coaxed out, Jim could let him have it.

'Pin!' he called softly. 'It's Jim. Sorry I'm so late back. You can come out now.'

A small bump on the duvet moved towards the pillow and Pin wriggled out.

'Hello,' he said, eyeing Jim doubtfully. 'Did you have a good time?'

'Yes,' replied Jim as he sat down on the bed. 'In fact it was one of the best birthdays I've ever had.'

'Good,' said Pin, looking serious.

'At least it was up to now,' added Jim and suddenly his hand shot out, grabbed Pin by the lapels of his jacket and held him up in front of his face.

'Yeek!' shrieked Pin, his eyes wide with shock. 'What are you doing? How dare you pick me up! Put me down at once, you ugly overgrown bully!' His face was white with anger and he waved his arms and legs in a frantic struggle to escape.

'Mind your manners,' growled Jim, 'and stop wriggling or I'll drop you on your silly head.' He held Pin higher to make the threat clearer.

Pin stopped struggling. 'What's wrong with you anyway?' he grumbled sulkily.

'What's wrong with me?' echoed Jim angrily. 'I'll tell you what's wrong with me. I've been blamed for something I didn't do and I've been sent to my room early, and all this on my birthday. What's more it's all your fault, as usual.'

'Sorry,' mumbled Pin. 'I didn't do much damage, really.'

'You did enough,' retorted Jim.

'It was an accident — well — a number of accidents,' replied Pin.

'Accidents seem to follow you around,' grumbled Jim. Then he sighed in exasperation. It was obviously ridiculous for a person of his size to physically threaten someone as small as Pin. He set him down on the bed beside him.

Pin straightened his jacket with a look of injured dignity on his face. Neither of them spoke for a while. Eventually Jim broke the silence.

'I'm sorry I threatened you,' he said.

'It's all right,' sighed Pin. 'You're not the first person to lose his temper with me. I'm sorry I've spoiled your birthday but I do have some excuse for what I did.'

'I know,' Jim admitted. 'I left you here on your own all day. I suppose you had to get something to eat and no doubt you were bored as well.'

'There's more to it than that,' Pin added sadly. 'Today was my birthday too.'

Jim suddenly felt as if the bed had fallen away below him.

'Oh Pin!' he gasped. 'I completely forgot. I was so taken up with my own birthday that I didn't even think ...' His voice trailed away. He felt so guilty and selfish he couldn't speak. He looked at Pin and saw a tiny tear trickle from his friend's eye. 'I really am sorry,' he whispered.

They were silent again for a while.

'I'm a hundred and twenty one today,' murmured Pin to himself.

'Happy birthday,' said Jim. Then he suddenly felt silly.

'Thanks,' sighed Pin.

In the silence that followed, the tinkling sounds of 'The

Last Rose of Summer' could be heard coming from Cat's room. Pin glanced quickly at Jim but he didn't seem to have noticed anything strange.

'Since it's your birthday we'll have to celebrate it,' announced Jim with sudden resolve. He stood up. 'Wait here,' he said. 'You've had enough exploring for one day.' Then he left the room.

Jim knew he was taking a risk. If his parents caught him he really would be in trouble, but his feeling of guilt made him daring. Very quietly he crept down the stairs. He could hear the familiar sound of the television newsreader through the sittingroom door. Luckily the kitchen door was open and the light was on. A floor-board creaked beneath his foot. Jim froze, waiting for the challenge of his father's voice. Nothing happened. He crept into the kitchen more quietly than a cat.

Jim knew exactly what he was looking for. The Jasmine House restaurant had provided a surprise cake for the party. There had been a good deal of it left over at the end of the meal because everyone had already been too well stuffed with beansprouts, noodles, water-chestnuts, sliced duckling in plum sauce and so on. The waiter had given Mrs Doran a box to take the rest of the birthday cake home. All Jim had to do now was find the cake and remove a slice for Pin.

He very quietly took a plate from the bottom press. Then he opened the top press and lifted down the cake tin. From the sittingroom he could hear the voice of the weather forecaster talking about bright spells and scattered showers. Once the forecast was over there would be a greater danger that someone would come out to the kitchen.

He knew the cake tin was noisy, so he had to ease the lid off very slowly. When he looked inside he found the tin was empty.

'Darn!' he whispered as he replaced the tin in the press.

His heart was beginning to thump now and his legs felt twitchy. He could hear the music for the end of the forecast and his father's voice saying something to his mother. Where was that cake? In the fridge of course! It was a cream cake.

In a few seconds he had a slice on the plate and the box back in its place. There was still one candle on the slice. Jim took a box of matches from the shelf and slipped it into his pocket. Then he 'borrowed' a bottle of lemonade from the press and made his getaway up the hall just as he heard the handle of the sittingroom door rattle behind him. As he went up the stairs two at a time he could hear his father filling the kettle in the kitchen. By the time he made it safely to his bedroom without meeting Cat or Eileen, he had decided he'd never be a burglar; the whole business was too nerve-racking.

Jim put his head around the bedroom door. 'Turn your back and don't look,' he whispered. Pin did as he was told. Jim stepped into the room and shut the door behind him. Then he struck a match, lit the candle and switched out the light. Instantly the room was filled with the soft mysterious flickering of candlelight. 'You can look now,' he called.

Pin turned round. When he saw the candle on the cake he clapped his hands with delight and his eyes gleamed in the reflected light of the flame. 'It's beautiful!' he cried.

Jim set the plate on his desk. Pin stood admiring it, warming his hands at the flame. Then he discovered that the shadow of his arms was making interesting shapes on the wall and Jim and himself were soon playing 'Guess the Shadow', a game that involved trying to make out the shadow-shapes made by each other. Pin proved to be very skilful, conjuring up eagles, mice, stags' heads, butterflies and even a birthday cake with a candle! Before they realised it the real candle was almost melted away.

'It's our custom to sing a birthday song while the candle is burning,' said Jim. 'Would you like to learn it?'

'Absolutely,' agreed Pin.

Jim softly sang 'Happy Birthday to You' and Pin repeated it in his light sweet voice. Line by line they went through the song. Pin had a good ear for music and got the tune right straight away. When they reached the end they sang it again together and Pin blew out the wavering flame on the candle stump just before it died.

Jim switched on his bedside light. 'Happy hundred and twenty first birthday, Pin,' he said.

'Happy eleventh birthday, Jim,' said Pin.

Jim cut the cake with his penknife and Pin sat down beside the plate and bravely attacked what to him was a cake-mountain. Then Jim opened the lemonade bottle, filled the cap and handed it to Pin.

'Your good health, Pin my friend, and may you have at least a hundred and twenty one more birthdays.'

'May you never have an unhappy one,' replied Pin, as he raised the brimming cap to his lips.

Jim drank from the bottle. Then they both sang 'Happy Birthday' again.

In the bedroom next to Jim's, Caitríona was lying on her bed staring at the jigsaw, the rubic cube, the music box and the bird. She let the incidents of the past two days play through her mind like a video, sometimes running it back to re-examine a particular incident, or playing through conversations frame by frame in slow-motion, or again fast forwarding to an interesting point, seeking a clue to the mystery.

She heard the singing in Jim's room dimly through the wall. 'Totally daft,' she muttered, thinking that Jim was singing 'Happy Birthday' to himself.

She went back to her puzzling and remembering. There was more to this than what had happened in her room. Jim's

alarm clock was working again and she certainly didn't believe the story about it falling and ending up fixed by accident. Then there was Jim's odd behaviour, or at least his
more-odd-than-usual behaviour, his conversations with the
vacuum and his slippers. Before that there was the strange
attraction of Matsa to Jim's pocket at breakfast yesterday
morning and Jim holding discussions aloud with himself
before he got up.

There was something peculiar going on and she felt sure
that Jim knew about it but wasn't telling. The 'Happy Birthday' singing started again beyond the wall. Suddenly
Caitríona sat bolt upright on her bed. Jim *had* told her! On
Saturday morning when she'd asked him who he was talking
to, he'd told her out straight, knowing she wouldn't believe
him. Pin!

For a few seconds she was overcome with excitement.
Then she immediately began to doubt herself. It couldn't be
true. But there was the jigsaw and the rubic cube and .... How
could she be sure? There had to be a way of testing Jim
without admitting that she knew. Once she was sure, she
would confront him with the evidence and demand to see the
little visitor. Caitríona's mind raced with excitement. Then
she hit on a very clever idea, so clever it was really simple.
She smiled to herself as she got up and headed for the door.

Jim and Pin were relaxing on the bed with stomachs full
of cream cake and lemonade, when they heard three soft taps
on the bedroom door. They glanced at each other, then Pin
calmly slipped under the duvet again while Jim went to open
the door. He wasn't too surprised when he saw Cat there but
he was surprised by what she said.

'Would you like to come into my room for a minute?' she
asked.

'But I'm not allowed,' replied Jim.

'It's all right if I ask you,' she said, 'and I want to show you something.'

Jim felt a moment's irritation at the interruption of his cosy celebration with Pin, but he was curious to find out what it was she wanted to show him. 'OK,' he agreed and he followed her into her room.

As Jim stood looking around at his sister's assembled treasures, Caitríona watched him carefully but he gave no sign that he was aware of anything out of the ordinary.

'What did you want to show me?' he asked.

'Look,' she said, pointing at the jigsaw.

Jim looked at it. It was quite an impressive picture, showing the towering castle with the thatched cottages of the folk park around it.

'How many pieces are in it?' he asked.

'Three thousand,' she replied.

'Wow!' exclaimed Jim. 'Well done. It must have taken you ages.'

Caitríona was watching his face like a hawk but there was still no sign. 'There's something else,' she said and she handed him the rubic cube.

Jim looked at the completed puzzle. He'd never even seen one finished before. 'That's fantastic,' he breathed. 'I really didn't think you'd be able to do it.'

'Neither did I,' replied Caitríona coolly.

There was a moment of silence. Jim was impressed with his sister's achievements but he was rather surprised that she should have asked him in to see them. Was she just showing off, or was she trying to be friendly because it was their birthday? He didn't know what she expected of him next.

'Well,' he said, 'I suppose I should be getting back to my room before Mam finds me here.'

'There's more,' said Caitríona quickly.

'More?' repeated Jim looking at her in surprise. She was certainly in a strange mood tonight.

'Listen!' she said as she lifted the lid on her music-box. The sweet tinkling of the Last Rose of Summer began as usual. Jim had heard it in the distance many times. He'd always liked that music-box and he wished someone had given one to him. Then he became aware that something was different. The tune was continuing longer than before and it was speeding up. He glanced at Caitríona, then he looked back at the box as the music became a frantic race. The sudden crack as the lid snapped shut made him jump.

'Did you fix it?' he asked, wondering if this was the latest in his sister's surprising achievements.

Caitríona gave him an odd look as if she suspected he was mocking her. 'I think it fixed itself,' she replied, staring at the box, 'just like your alarm clock.' Her voice was heavy with suggested disbelief.

Jim began to feel uneasy. He sensed that Caitríona was about to spring a surprise on him and knowing her it was unlikely to be pleasant.

'Isn't it extraordinary?' she insisted.

'Absolutely,' agreed Jim as he began to edge towards the door.

But Caitríona wasn't finished yet. 'Hold on,' she said. 'There's something even more amazing.'

'What next?' wondered Jim as he watched her pick up the bird.

'Look!' she commanded, as she turned the key and set the bird free on her dressing-table.

Jim still felt guilty about having broken that bird. He eyed it with a feeling of dread and a suspicion that this would turn out to be some sort of long-delayed revenge on him for his wrong-doing. He wasn't at all prepared to see the bird stepping across the dressing-table, pecking happily and cheeping merrily and he was quite astounded by the acrobatics at the end, even if the creature did look a bit undignified lying on its back waving its legs in the air.

Caitríona picked the bird up and set it carefully on its feet. 'What do you think of that?' she asked.

'Absolutely amazing,' he replied and he meant it. Now he really wanted to escape from his sister's room. Deep in his stomach he had a panicky feeling that Cat was about to pounce.

'I'll tell you something even more amazing,' said Caitríona lowering her voice. 'I didn't complete the jigsaw and I didn't solve the rubic cube. I certainly couldn't have fixed the music-box or the bird. What's more, I've no idea who did. It was all done when I got home yesterday after the shopping. I think the person who stole my chocolates did it.'

Jim looked at her open-mouthed. 'This is incredible,' he said.

'Yes it is,' she agreed. 'It's the most incredible thing that has ever happened to me.'

'Anyway, I'm glad your bird is working again,' said Jim, 'even if it is a mystery. And thanks for showing it to me.' Before Caitríona could reply, he escaped to his room.

Caitríona picked up the bird. 'Now Birdie,' she whispered. 'All we have to do is wait and see what he does or what he doesn't do.'

7   The Burglar

Jim intended having another rough session with Pin when he got back to his room but the little man was curled up in the bed fast asleep. He didn't feel he could reasonably waken Pin up, so he got ready for bed and after reading for a while, he switched out the bedside light and fell asleep himself.

Several hours later, Pin woke up. He didn't know why but he felt a sense of alarm. In the dark the clock-face glowed, showing two-thirty. Pin listened. Jim's steady breathing was all he heard. He lay back on the pillow and was about to doze off again when he heard a sound from the back garden and he knew why he had woken up. Quietly he eased himself out from under the duvet and slid skilfully down to the floor. He had just reached the open bedroom door when he heard a clink of metal followed by a 'Shh!'

Jim sighed heavily in his sleep and turned over.

'Enemies?' muttered Pin. He wondered if he should wake Jim up and tell him, but he had caused so much trouble for his friend already that he wanted to be sure. Pin listened intently at the bedroom door. No one else seemed to have noticed the sound.

He decided to investigate on his own.

Quietly he slipped across the landing and slid downstairs faster than a frightened mouse. The door between the hallway and the sittingroom was open. Pin looked inside. The room was dark but at the far end a beam of torchlight played along the window. Pin could see the outline of a head beside the torch. Someone was definitely trying to break in!

Realising that these enemies were too dangerous for him to deal with, Pin decided to be sensible and wake up Jim. He turned to go and found himself staring into two glowing green eyes. Matsa was looming over him. She blinked slowly. Then she opened her mouth and miaowed, showing her moist pink tongue and sharp white teeth.

Pin took one look at the puzzled animal, leaped back and slammed the sittingroom door in the cat's face. He stood in the dark with his heart thudding inside him and leaned against the door for support. His legs were trembling. Before he had time to recover himself, he was startled by a sharp crack and a shower of tinkling glass, as the back window was smashed. The torch beam inspected the shattered pane, then a hand reached in through the hole and undid the window catch.

Pin raced across the floor to the kitchen door but it was firmly shut. The window was open now and a bulky shape appeared on the ledge, grunting with the effort of climbing in. Pin darted over to the couch and leaped up onto the cushion. From there he climbed onto the bookshelves and hid in a small 'cave' below a book that was leaning against the shelf end.

The burglar landed with a thud on the floor. Pin could hear

his heavy breathing. Then a second smaller figure appeared
in the window and eased himself lightly into the room.

'An older giant and a younger one,' thought Pin to himself.
'They're not very good at this either. They make too much
noise.'

Good at it or not, Pin knew he wouldn't stand a chance if
they discovered him. Luckily they didn't turn on the light but
examined the room with their torch. Then they started opening presses and drawers, rummaging about and scattering
stuff carelessly on the floor. The younger one had a bag and
they put some things in it, though Pin couldn't see what they
were taking. The older one was working his way along the
room towards the bookshelves were Pin was hiding. It would
only be a matter of time before all the books would end up
on the floor.

Pin was afraid, but his fear was quickly turning to anger.
Just who did these people think they were? How dare they
break into his friend's home and take things that were part of
the family's personal lives? This was an attack on his friends.

Pin's blood boiled with rage and his mind raced. He had
to raise the alarm but how could he get out of the room with
both doors closed and two enemy giants on the loose? If only
that darn cat hadn't turned up and frightened the life out of
him.

His eyes were getting used to the dark now and he looked
frantically around hoping to find something that might help
him.

Just then the the older giant pulled a drawer out of a press
and emptied the contents out on the floor. As he did so the
torch beam accidentally flickered across the room, glancing
along the mantlepiece. The beam of light moved quickly, but
Pin's eyes were equally fast. He saw the remote control for
the television among Jim and Cat's birthday cards and a

daring plan formed in his mind.

While the giants were busy sorting out their loot, Pin dropped from his shelf onto the arm of the couch. There he paused. A wide chasm lay between him and the mantlepiece. If his jump failed he would split his skull on the stone fireplace below. He stepped back and took a deep breath. Then calling up all his strength, he ran to the edge of the arm of the couch and sprang into the air. For a heart-stopping second he thought he was going to miss, then his feet hit a birthday card and he landed right beside the remote control. He didn't wait to see if the giants had noticed him but instantly stepped on the On button.

The burglars heard the noise of the falling card but they didn't have time to investigate it, for the sittingroom was suddenly filled with the sound of clanging electric guitars, pounding drums and wailing saxophones. Pin had found the Music Channel!

'Bloody hell!' cursed the older giant. 'Kill that thing!'

Before the younger one could switch it off, Pin stamped on the volume control so that for a few seconds the room was as loud as a disco. Then he dodged back behind a birthday card. Meanwhile the smaller giant had reached the set and while both of them were distracted by their unexpected bout of modern entertainment, Pin leaped onto the couch again.

By the time the television was switched off, Pin had reached the hall door without being seen. The burglars stood like dark statues in the middle of the floor listening, ready to take flight. Pin heard Matsa miaow again outside the door and plan number two flashed into his mind. He made two claws of his hands and scratched fiercely on the door. Then he drew in a huge breath and released an enormous bark!

The burglars leaped in the air with fright. Pin scratched and barked and scratched and barked for all he was worth.

'It's a flaming Alsatian!' squeaked the younger one. Both of them raced for the window. The older burglar got there first but the younger one pushed him aside and jumped onto the windowsill. He was in such a hurry that he cracked his skull against the window frame but before he had time to recover, his companion shoved him angrily from behind and he fell in a heap into the garden. While the fat giant struggled to escape, Pin scratched and barked again and again. He was enjoying himself now.

Meanwhile upstairs, Jim had been awakened by a sudden blast of pop-music. He jerked up in bed, switched on his light and looked for Pin.

'Oh no!' he groaned, when he realised his friend wasn't there. 'Not again!'

The music grew suddenly louder, then cut off abruptly. Jim dived out of bed, grabbed his dressing-gown and hurried to the door. On the landing he almost ran into his father who was heading for the stairs with a hurling-stick in his hand. Jim's Mam was hurrying after him, struggling to put on her dressing-gown and muttering, 'Be careful Tom, they may be dangerous!'

'Not half as dangerous as I'll be!' retorted the furious Mr Doran.

Eileen and Caitríona appeared at their bedroom doors.

'Stay up here!' commanded Mrs Doran as she followed her husband down the stairs.

Then the barking started. Matsa shot up the stairs as if she was on fire and vanished into the bathroom. Everyone froze in astonishment! Even the furious Mr Doran hesitated to burst into the sittingroom when there was obviously a savage dog attacking the door in its rage to get out and tear him apart.

'Phone the Gardaí!' whispered Mrs Doran, and that's exactly what Mr Doran did. Jim stood on the stairs with Eileen and Caitríona and wondered what had become of Pin. Was he in the room with the burglars? Had the dog killed him? They heard the sound of scuffling and the burglars cursing at each other. Someone cried out in pain.

'What on earth is going on in there?' muttered Mrs Doran. 'Who are they attacking?'

Meanwhile Tom Doran had got through to the Gardaí. As it happened there was a patrol car not far off and the Gardaí were quickly on the scene. Two officers ran around the side of the house, saw the burglars climbing over the garden wall and went after them.

Another Garda arrived on a motor bike and Mrs Doran let him in the front door. Tom Doran quickly explained about the noises and the dog. The Garda looked at him in surprise. Then he threw the sittingroom door open and switched on the light. The room was empty: there was no dog and no burglars.

The others followed him in. The room was in a mess. Books, papers, cutlery, tablecloths and ornaments were scattered over the floor. A chilly breeze blew in through the open shattered window.

'Don't touch anything,' advised the Garda. 'We'll have to check for fingerprints.' He examined the open window. Then he picked up the burglars' bag from the floor. 'Seems they left in a hurry,' he remarked. 'Very strange.'

'Most peculiar,' agreed Tom Doran.

Mary Doran's face was a thunderstorm. 'The dirty thieves!' she exclaimed. 'Look at the mess they've made of my sittingroom.'

'They always do that,' replied the Garda sympathetically. 'In fact it's usually worse. We'll check to see if anything has been taken once the fingerprinting is done. I'll have to get a statement from both of you, if you don't mind.'

'Of course,' said Mr Doran.

'I think we could all do with a cup of tea,' said Mary Doran and she headed into the kitchen. Everyone followed except Jim. He was looking anxiously around the room for any sign of Pin when he felt a gentle tug at the leg of his pyjamas. Looking down he saw his friend standing on the floor beside an armchair. Jim crouched down and picked him up.

'Are you all right?' he whispered.

'Yes,' replied Pin. 'I'll explain it all later.'

Jim nodded and quietly slipped him into his pocket.

'Jim, do you want some tea?' called Mary Doran from the kitchen door.

'Yes please,' replied Jim and he went into the kitchen, though he was really more interested in being part of the excitement than in drinking tea.

Everyone was sitting around the table. There was a plate of biscuits in the middle. Mrs Doran was pouring steaming hot tea into mugs and Eileen had just put two slices of bread in the toaster. The Garda was talking to Mr Doran and taking notes.

'Do you mean they actually turned on the television?' he asked, looking very doubtful.

'So it seemed,' replied Tom Doran. 'We all heard a blast of pop-music and it was pretty loud too.'

'It was the music that woke me up,' put in Caitríona, in support of her father's evidence.

'I've never heard of burglars playing music while they robbed a house,' said the Garda, 'especially when the family was upstairs. Of course, they might have thought you were all away.'

'That seems unlikely with the car parked in the driveway,' objected Tom Doran.

'True,' agreed the Garda. 'Maybe they were drunk.'

Jim sat down between Eileen and his mother. He took a biscuit, broke a piece off and slipped it into his pocket.

As he felt Pin take it from his hand he thought he heard a muffled snigger coming from his pocket. He wondered what Pin could find so funny.

'And you're all certain about this dog?' continued the Garda, looking around the table as if he hoped they would say they weren't.

'Absolutely,' said Mary Doran. 'And it sounded like a big one, an Alsatian or a Rottweiler at least.'

'That's even more incredible,' sighed the Garda as he shook his head from side to side. 'Burglars tend to be chased out of houses by guard dogs. They don't usually bring them with them.' He stared at his note book. Obviously he was afraid that his report would be laughed out of court.

Inside the pocket of his dressing-gown, Jim could feel Pin shaking with silent laughter. Clearly there was more to this incident than met the eye or indeed the ear.

'You haven't noticed any other strange activity around the house recently?' asked the Garda.

From the other side of the table Caitríona gave Jim a knowing glare. He looked away from her.

'No,' replied Tom Doran. 'Everything here has been quite normal.'

Just then the toaster clattered noisily and two golden slices of bread shot out of it and sailed over the table. One splashed down in Caitríona's tea, the other landed expertly on the plate in front of the Garda. He stared at it for a moment, then looked uneasily at Mr and Mrs Doran.

'Well, that's rather handy,' he remarked.

Suddenly everyone around the table burst into a storm of uncontrollable laughter.

Jim didn't even bother to look at Caitríona.

8   Masher Moran's Madness

'If I bring you to school with me, you'll have to swear by the Seniors that you'll stay out of sight and not interfere with anything,' declared Jim.

It was Monday morning and Jim was in his room packing his books and lunch into his schoolbag. He wasn't in the best of humour. All the disturbance of the night before had left him short of sleep. He'd half hoped that the interrupted burglary could be used as an excuse for taking a day off school, especially as the day was a Monday. His mother would have none of it though.

'I'm not having you hanging around here all day under my feet,' she'd said. 'I'll have enough to do cleaning up the sittingroom after those blackguards, and besides the glazier will be coming to put in the window. If you're feeling tired then you can go to bed early tonight.'

That was the end of the argument.

Now Pin had announced that he couldn't bear another day

alone. Jim had tried to explain what school was like but Pin insisted he'd be able to take care of himself.

'On the honour of the Seniors,' Pin promised solemnly. 'I'll keep myself out of trouble.'

'All right,' sighed Jim. 'At least I'll be able to keep an eye on you when you're with me instead of having you getting into mischief at home.'

'Oh now, be fair!' exclaimed Pin. 'What about last night?'

'You were brilliant last night,' Jim agreed. 'You saved the house and you were very clever. For that, I'll forgive you everything you've done up to now. What happens from now on is different. Today is a new day *and* it's a Monday. I'm going to have enough trouble without you adding to it.'

'What's so terrible about Mondays?' Pin asked.

'Every Monday morning we have a gym lesson,' replied Jim gloomily. 'A special teacher comes in to do it with us.'

'So what's the worry? Gymnastics is fun,' said Pin.

'Fun?' exclaimed Jim. 'Not with Attila the Bun it isn't.'

'Is that his real name?' asked Pin.

'Of course not, you daft idiot,' replied Jim. 'That's what we call him. It started out as Attila the Hun, who was a famous savage warrior of long ago. We reckon our gym master must be related to him because of the way he treats us. Anyway, he takes a drink of tea from his flask at the end of the lesson while we're getting changed and we noticed that he always has a bun with it. One day John Callan, the class joker, called him Attila the Bun and the name stuck.'

'Is he really all that bad?' asked Pin.

'He's all right with the ones who are good at gym,' replied Jim. 'But he gets really impatient and sarcastic with the rest.'

'I take it that you're one of the rest,' said Pin.

'Not just one of them,' Jim moaned. 'I'm the worst of them. As soon as I walk into the gym my legs and arms go all wobbly and I start falling over things. I don't know why, but I'm worse in the gym than anywhere else. If he asked me to walk from one end of the room to the other I don't think I could do it without a disaster. Then he starts making fun of me. I wouldn't mind that so much if it wasn't for Masher Moran and his mob.'

'Masher Moran?' repeated Pin, with his eyebrows raised. 'Is he another ancient savage warrior?'

'No,' said Jim. 'He's a modern savage bully. Whatever the Bun calls me in the gym, Masher repeats with his own improvements in the schoolyard. It's no fun being laughed at when you're not strong enough to do anything about it. If he's in a particularly sour humour he thumps me as well.'

'Now I understand why you hate Mondays,' murmured Pin thoughtfully.

'And I hope you understand how important it is that Masher doesn't see you,' added Jim.

'Oh I do! I do!' agreed Pin with feeling.

'Right,' said Jim. 'I think the best place for you is in my schoolbag. You'll have a bit of space to stretch your legs and you won't be as likely to suffocate or be squashed as in my pocket.'

'Fair enough,' agreed Pin and he hopped in beside the cellophane bag that held Jim's lunch. Jim closed his schoolbag and headed downstairs.

Jim and Caitríona left the house together but long before they reached the school she had paired off with her friend Laura O'Toole and a group of other girls. When Jim got to the schoolyard three boys from his class were kicking a ball around.

'Hey Jim!' called Joe McGlinn. 'We're goin' to have a match. Put your bag down for the goalpost.'

Normally Jim would have been glad enough to join in, but

the thought of Pin being trampled underfoot made him hesitate.

'I don't think I want to,' he replied.

'Ah come on,' begged Tony Ryan. 'We need the fourth goalpost.'

'I can't,' answered Jim unhappily.

Suddenly his bag was wrenched from his hand. He spun around and found himself facing the large grinning face of Masher Moran.

'Are we in bad humour this morning, Tinchy?' sneered Masher.

'Give me my bag, Moran,' demanded Jim.

'It's not your bag,' retorted Masher. 'It's our goalpost. Isn't it lads?'

'That's right,' chorused the others. In the schoolyard everyone always agreed with Masher.

Paul Garland and John Callan came in through the gate. Masher's gang was gathering as if he'd organised it deliberately.

'Hey lads,' he called. 'Tinchy is donating his schoolbag for our goalposts. Isn't he a good sport?'

'Oh he's real decent,' agreed Callan. 'Maybe he'd like to offer himself as the football as well.'

They all laughed. Jim cursed his luck. If he had been a few seconds later, they'd have had their goalposts and their game under way and he'd have been left alone. But his anger was giving him courage and he was determined that he wasn't going to let them use his bag, even if he had to fight the whole lot of them on his own.

'You're not using my bag,' he shouted.

'Why not Tinchy?' Masher replied. 'Is it a special bag? Is it different from our bags? Maybe it's magic.'

Jim leaped forward and snatched at the bag. He almost got

it, but Masher stepped back just in time and before Jim could stop him he threw the schoolbag to John Callan.

'It is magic!' exclaimed Callan. 'Look, it flies!' And he threw it over Jim's head to Joe McGlinn.

Jim made a move towards McGlinn but he tossed it to Masher again. 'This is a better game than football,' shouted McGlinn.

The thought of Pin inside the bag being thrown around enraged Jim. He flung himself at Masher in a wild fury.

The bully pushed him off so forcefully that Jim staggered backwards and fell, cutting his elbow.

Sensing that Jim was in a serious temper, Masher Moran decided to put the bag beyond his reach. 'Let's see if it can fly to the roof,' he called and to Jim's horror he threw the bag high into the air.

'You'll hurt him!' screamed Jim, too distressed to think of what he was saying.

The bag landed with a thud on the flat roof of the school toilets.

'Him?' repeated Masher. 'What have you got in there, a pet hamster?'

'Mind your own bloody business!' roared Jim.

'He *has* got something in there,' said McGlinn. 'So that's why he wouldn't let us use it.'

Too late Jim realised his mistake. Already Moran was standing on a window-ledge and reaching for a drainpipe. It was against school rules of course but the boys often climbed up that way to rescue footballs from the roof. With a feeling of rising panic, Jim scrambled up from the ground and sprang at Masher, grabbing him by the leg. The bully clung on to the drainpipe and tried to kick Jim off. Then Callan and Garland gripped Jim's arms and tore him from Moran.

Inside the bag, Pin was recovering from his ordeal. He had

been cushioned from the main force of his crash-landing on the roof by Jim's lunch bag. He wasn't badly hurt, though the sandwiches were in a bit of a mess. Pin had heard a good deal of the conversation before the throwing started and he knew who was behind the trouble. If Jim was angry, then Pin was furious. He crawled over the squashed lunch and across some books and managed to squeeze himself out through an opening in the top of the bag. He found himself on a flat black roof covered with gravel. There were a number of small pools of water lying there, as well as a burst ball and an old boot.

From the shouts and noises below, Pin gathered that Masher was about to climb up onto the roof. Quickly Pin crept to the edge and peeped over. Masher's head was directly below him and rising. Pin ducked back and looked around. Anger made his brain work faster. He darted over to the old boot and tried to pick it up. To his surprise it was too heavy to lift. He looked inside it and discovered it was full of rainwater.

'Good,' muttered Pin. 'That will be even better.'

He got behind the boot and pushed furiously until he had it positioned directly above the drainpipe. Then he tilted the boot on its toe and shoved the whole lot down on top of the bully.

If the children below were surprised to see a boot leaping off the roof, Masher Moran was even more surprised to receive the full weight of it on his face, while icy water drenched his hair and flooded down the neck of his shirt.

Pin's efforts were rewarded by a shriek from the bully and a string of very rude curses. But he wasn't the only one who heard what Masher said. The school Principal, Mrs O'Connor, had come out of the main door at that very moment. She not only heard Masher's interesting language, she saw him clinging to the drainpipe below the roof as well.

'Rory Moran!' she called angrily. 'Come down from there at once. You know very well you're strictly forbidden to climb on that roof. Get inside to the office.'

Mrs O'Connor wasn't the kind of teacher you argued with. Masher was escorted away in disgrace. The instant Mrs O'Connor appeared, Callan and Garland released Jim's arms and melted into the crowd. Their loyalty to Masher did not stretch to sharing punishment with him.

Just then the bell rang and everyone ran off to line up for their classes. Jim found himself standing alone below the roof, wondering if he dared climb up to see what state Pin was in and to get his schoolbag back. Then he heard a light scraping sound above him and looking up he saw his school-bag appearing at the edge of the roof. Jim glanced quickly about him. There was no one else around to witness the strange scene.

'Pin!' he called. 'I'm directly below you.'

With that, the bag was pushed off the roof and landed in Jim's arms. Then Pin's head appeared.

'Do you think you could catch me like that?' he called.

'Of course I can!' answered Jim.

Without a second's hesitation, Pin leaped off the roof. Jim caught him neatly in both his hands.

'Pin!' he exclaimed. 'You're a little wonder!'

'I really enjoyed giving that guy the boot,' said Pin with a wicked grin.

'We'll have to hurry or I'll be in trouble for being late into class,' said Jim. 'I think you might be safer in my pocket this time.'

'Agreed,' replied Pin.

Jim placed him carefully in the breast pocket of his jacket, leaving the flap open. Then he hurried to join his class and caught up with the end of his line just as they were going through the classroom door.

Once inside, everyone was quiet. Jim's teacher, Miss Lynch, was pleasant but firm with her pupils. She created an atmosphere of calm order in her room that Jim liked.

He slipped gratefully into his seat and glanced around him. Pat Duffy, the boy who usually sat beside him, was absent. Jim was glad not to have anyone too close to him just then, though he liked Pat.

Masher's place was empty as well. The Principal must be giving him a roasting down in the office. Jim hoped that he wouldn't be drawn into the trouble. Masher was a genius at inventing complicated excuses for himself that usually involved other people in his misfortunes.

'We will start with a maths test this morning,' announced Miss Lynch. 'This is mental work so just write down the answers.'

As Jim began to open his schoolbag he glanced over at Caitríona and discovered she was looking at him with more than usual interest. He guessed she'd heard about the incident outside. When he reached into his bag for his maths copy, his fingers found a sticky mess. His plastic lunch bag had burst and his favourite date and banana sandwiches were adding flavour and colour to his copies. He hoped Miss Lynch wouldn't object too much. Anyway he could tell her that Masher was responsible for the mess. Then it occurred to him that she might want to know how he got his schoolbag down again. He could hardly tell her that it had jumped off the roof into his arms. He decided to leave Masher out of the story and tell her his lunch had burst.

Miss Lynch ran a weekly competition in her class, the winning team being let off homework at the weekend. The results of the mental maths tests would be called out and each pupil's score added to the team's total. Jim usually scored five or six out of ten, but this morning he discovered he had an unexpected advantage.

Miss Lynch began to call out the problems and Jim wrote his answers as neatly as he could on his banana-flavoured maths copy. As the test progressed Jim felt Pin straighten up inside his pocket. Then the unbuttoned flap moved slightly. When Jim wrote the third answer, a tiny quiet voice that no one but himself could hear, whispered, 'Have you forgotten how to multiply decimals by a hundred?' Jim checked his answer and found he'd left out the decimal point. He quickly put it in.

Pin said nothing again until the seventh question. 'She said percentage, not decimal, dopey head!' he grumbled. Jim quickly converted his decimal to the required percentage. Pin made him revise the answer to the eighth as well. Jim did the rest on his own.

During the remainder of the lesson Pin kept a look-out from the vantage point of Jim's pocket. Whenever there was any risk of someone seeing him, he lowered his head and peeped out through the button-hole. Masher Moran returned to the class with a rather red face and Pin noted him carefully as he made his way to his seat not far from Jim's desk.

'I'll get you for this, Tinchy,' Masher muttered as he sat down.

'Rory Moran,' called Miss Lynch. 'Did you say something?'

'No Miss,' lied Masher.

'I hope not,' replied Miss Lynch. 'You're in enough trouble as it is and I'm not going to put up with any of your nonsense.'

'Yes Miss,' agreed Rory, though the scowl on his face said otherwise.

The results of the mental maths test were called out. For the first time ever Jim scored ten out of ten. He got a round

of applause from his team and found it hard to look innocently modest while everyone was looking at him. He knew
he'd have enjoyed it more if he'd achieved the score by
himself. Pin didn't make him feel any better by giving his ribs
a gentle dig with his elbow.

'Well done, Jim,' Miss Lynch said. 'I hope you'll be able to
keep up this high standard from now on.'

'I'll try, Miss,' Jim replied uneasily, as he realised that once
again Pin's 'help' had landed him in an awkward situation.
'Thanks a lot, friend,' he muttered to his pocket.

'Don't mention it,' came the tiny reply.

The maths lesson was almost over when Pin thought of a
magnificent way to take his revenge on Masher Moran. It was
such a great idea, he just had to do it right away, in spite of
his promise to Jim.

While every head in the class was bent over their copies
and every pen was busy taking down the homework that
Miss Lynch was writing on the blackboard, the silence was
broken by Masher Moran's voice saying, 'This is a really
stupid homework!'

Everyone, including the astonished Masher, gasped at the
sheer cheek of this remark. Every head turned and every eye
in the class stared at him in disbelief. Miss Lynch turned from
the blackboard and fixed the scarlet-faced Masher with a look
that should have turned him to stone.

'So you think this work is stupid, Rory Moran?' she asked
icily.

'Yes Miss, I — I mean no Miss,' stammered Masher.

'You've already had one warning, Master Moran,' she
continued, her voice growing more angry as she spoke. 'If I
hear as much as a whisper out of you for the rest of the day
you'll end up at Mrs O'Connor's office again. As for the
"stupid" homework, you can write it out twice tonight!'

'B-But Miss I...' spluttered Masher.

'No buts!' snapped Miss Lynch. 'Get to the back of the class.'

Jim bent his head over his copy so that no one could see his face. Inside his breast pocket he could feel Pin shaking with silent laughter.

The class returned to their work. A bewildered Rory Moran gathered up his books and stumbled towards the back of the room. He couldn't understand why everything was going wrong for him today. He didn't know that his troubles were only starting. He had just passed Jim's table when the impossible happened again. From somewhere quite near him he heard his own voice say, 'I'm not doing this stupid home-work for you.'

Masher was so surprised he dropped half his books on the floor.

For a moment the class was stunned into silence, then someone began to giggle hysterically. Miss Lynch rose from her desk. She stood there, white-faced and tight-lipped, while her eyes bored into Masher's face. Then she erupted.

'Rory Moran!' she thundered. 'How dare you speak to me in such an insolent manner. Never in all my days in school have I come across such downright cheek. In addition to the double homework you have already been given, you will now write one hundred lines and you will report to Mrs O'Connor's office at the eleven o'clock break.'

'But I didn't do anything!' protested Masher.

'Do not add barefaced lies to your already disgraceful behaviour,' retorted the angry Miss Lynch. 'Every pupil in this class heard what you said.'

A murmur of agreement ran through the class and heads nodded in support of the teacher's statement.

Rory Moran stared wildly around the room as if he expected

that someone would come to his rescue but most of the children were not a bit sorry to see the bully land himself in trouble and even his closest followers thought that this time he had gone too far.

'I tell you I didn't do anything,' insisted Masher. 'It wasn't me who said that. Someone is trying to get me into trouble.'

'Don't be ridiculous child,' snapped Miss Lynch. 'You don't need anyone's help to get yourself into trouble, you do that very well on your own.'

The other children laughed their agreement.

Even when he was guilty, Masher Moran could hardly bring himself to accept punishment. Now he was being blamed in the wrong in front of the whole class and they were actually laughing at him! An enormous rage swept through him and he lost his head completely. He flung his books into the air and leaped up and down, pounding his feet on the floor like a three-year-old having a tantrum.

'You stupid woman!' he screamed at the teacher. 'I didn't do it! Can't you understand that, you silly old cow?'

No one laughed. Miss Lynch didn't shout back at him. In fact no one was even looking at him. When Masher turned his head he saw the reason why. Mrs O'Connor was standing in the doorway. She didn't speak. She beckoned to Masher with her finger.

The walk to the classroom door was like a nightmare. Masher felt as if his legs had turned to jelly. He stumbled and had to grab hold of a table for support. In the deathly silence his heart thundered so loudly that the sound seemed to fill the whole room. He was totally bewildered. How on earth had all this happened to him?

Mrs O'Connor stood aside to let Masher walk past, then she nodded quietly to Miss Lynch, stepped outside and closed the door behind her.

A sigh of relief escaped from the class.

'You may start your break now,' Miss Lynch said quietly.

☙

On the way out to the yard Jim slipped into the toilet and locked the door behind him. He lifted the flap of his breast pocket and looked at the naughty smiling face that peeped slyly up at him.

'You clever little rascal!' laughed Jim.

'It was nothing,' Pin said modestly. 'He deserved it and he made the whole thing a lot worse for himself. I imagine that fellow has got away with much more than he has ever been punished for.'

'You're right about that,' agreed Jim. 'By the way, what happened to that promise of yours not to interfere?'

'Ah,' sighed Pin. 'Well, he interfered with me first. I didn't enjoy being used as a flying parcel. Anyway, would you rather it hadn't happened?'

'Of course not,' grinned Jim. 'Just be careful. You're lucky no one realised what was happening.'

'Not lucky,' smirked Pin. 'Just very skilful.'

When Jim joined the other children in the schoolyard he found that the incident with his schoolbag had been completely forgotten in the excitement over Masher's outburst. No one said anything about the strange boot that had jumped off the roof all by itself and no one thought to ask him how he'd got his bag back.

News of Masher's madness spread like wildfire through the school. As the story flew from mouth to mouth it grew more amazing in the telling. One version had him dancing on the tables and tearing his books to shreds. Another said he'd run down the corridor and kicked Mrs O'Connor's door. Yet another claimed he'd kicked Mrs O'Connor.

'Masher was always a bit of a lunatic anyway,' said Paul Garland, who was anxious to make it clear that he wasn't backing Masher in this latest escapade.

'Yeah,' agreed Tony Ryan. 'I think he's flipped his lid this time. I heard they're sending him to a psychiatrist to have his head examined.'

Jim listened but said nothing. Laura O'Toole and Caitríona came over to them.

'They say Masher's being expelled,' said Laura. 'Serve him right too.'

Caitríona looked suspiciously at Jim but she said nothing.

Just then Masher's father came striding in through the school gate and headed towards the Principal's office. By the time the bell rang for the end of break, everyone was certain that Masher Moran was either expelled forever or on his way to a lunatic asylum.

9 Attila the Bun

No one could remember having such an entertaining morning in school before. They'd even forgotten that they were to have their gym lesson with Attila the Bun next. The girls changed into their tracksuits in the classroom. The boys were sent to the hall to change. There was a row of coat-hooks at the back of the hall where the boys hung up their clothes. Jim was deliberately slow in changing. When all the others had moved away, he carefully hung up his jacket so that Pin could see what was going on in the hall. Then he leaned close to the pocket and whispered, 'Keep out of sight and don't try any funny stuff.'

'Of course not,' replied Pin. 'Relax.'

'Relax,' muttered Jim. 'That's a laugh.'

The rest of the boys had gathered at the other end of the hall and the girls were coming in through the doorway. Attila the Bun strode in through them with his head in the air and went to the end of the room where the coats were hanging.

He left a plastic bag that held his flask and the famous bun on a windowsill. Then he took off his duffel coat and hung it up. He was wearing a green tracksuit decorated with red diamond patches along the seams. Ignoring the children at the other end of the room, he began to do his own warm-up exercises.

'Just look at him,' muttered Tony Ryan. 'He's a champion show-off.'

'And a world-class mouth,' added Joe McGlinn.

Even those who were good at gym weren't too enthusiastic about spending an hour under the Bun's authority. Attila, in fact, was an excellent gymnast and he was very good at organising his lessons and keeping strict control over the class. His problem was that he really didn't like most of the children, especially the boys. He had always been good at gym and had won medals and passed all his exams without any trouble at all. He couldn't understand how some children, no matter how hard they tried, just couldn't get things right. Whenever a handstand collapsed, Attila thought it was done on purpose. If a fearful child held up the rest of the group waiting their turn to vault over the horse, Attila thought the boy was deliberately upsetting his well-planned lesson in order to make him look foolish. He was afraid that if his lessons didn't run to plan, he'd lose control and everything would fall apart. This made him very impatient with those who weren't good at gym and he showed his annoyance by making fun of them. It never really occurred to him that his victims might feel hurt by what he said, or that others in the class might take his remarks as a signal that they should bully the victim. The one who suffered most from this was Jim.

Attila found the girls a lot easier to deal with. It wasn't so much that they were better at gym than the boys, but he felt less threatened by them.

His favourite was a tall girl called Mary Furlong and though Attila would never have admitted it, she was definitely his pet. Mary was an attractive girl, with long fair hair, blue eyes and smooth skin. Several of the boys in the class fancied her, and she was also excellent at gymnastics. Of course it wasn't her fault that Attila liked her but the gym master's attentions had made her a bit of a show-off and she was definitely not popular among the other girls in the class.

Attila leaped up onto an old vaulting horse that was kept at the end of the hall near the coat hooks. He blew a shrill blast on his whistle and all talk stopped.

'Groups!' he shouted and everyone hurried into their proper line.

'Group One begin with the vaulting horse,' called Attila. 'Group Two do cartwheels on the mats. Group Three begin with the climbing frame. Group Four, you will be doing something new today — juggling with beanbags. Places!' He blew another blast on his whistle and everyone ran to the proper part of the hall.

Each group began its activity while Attila moved from one to the other making sure that everything was being done exactly as he had taught them. Jim was in Group Four and so was Mary Furlong. Attila began by demonstrating how to juggle two bags. He was really good at it and the bags flew so quickly it was difficult to see how he did it. Then he made each child in the group do it on their own. Tony Ryan went first but he dropped a bag straight away.

'How's your eyesight, boy?' remarked Attila as he took the bags and showed them again.

Pat O'Toole did a little better. Then it was Mary's turn.

She managed two throws before one bag fell to the floor.

'Quite good,' smiled Attila. 'Try it again.'

This time Mary kept it going for five throws.

'Excellent,' beamed the Bun. 'You have a quick eye and a fine pair of hands.'

Jim was next in line. Attila looked at him as if he was something disgusting that the cleaners had forgotten to take away. 'Ah, Doran,' he sighed. 'I suppose you might as well have a try.'

Jim had been carefully studying what everyone else was doing. He thought he understood it, but as soon as he took the bags in his hands, his mind panicked and he couldn't picture what to do at all.

'Well, get on with it,' snapped Attila. 'We want you to do it today.'

Jim threw both bags in the air at once, then tried in vain to snatch at them before they fell. One sailed over his head and hit Joe McGlinn on the ear. The other landed in a waste bin standing nearby.

'Oh very good, very good indeed,' mocked the Bun, while the others sniggered. 'Why don't you hop into the bin yourself and stay there with the rest of the rubbish.' He took the bags and gave them to Mary Furlong again. 'Now watch how Mary does it.'

Mary did ten perfect throws.

'That's juggling,' said Attila warmly. 'The rest of you get your own beanbags from the equipment box and copy Mary. Just watch how Mary does it.' He went off then to supervise the cartwheels.

'I didn't know it was bin day Jim,' sniggered Joe McGlinn.

'Jim couldn't catch a cold,' tittered Laura O'Toole.

Jim ignored them and got on with practising his juggling. He had just managed to get two throws in without dropping a bag when the whistle blew.

'Change!' shouted the Bun and everyone left what they

were doing and ran to the next piece of equipment.

For Jim's group that meant the climbing frame. This was made up of two metal frames with a ladder stretching between them about two and a half metres above the ground. They lined up and each in turn had to climb up the frame, grip the ladder and work their way across hanging from the rungs. By the time Jim's turn came, his legs were quaking so much that he could scarcely climb up the frame. Somehow he reached the top and with his heart in his mouth, launched himself into space. By sheer will-power and courage he managed to get almost half-way across the ladder. Then his strength failed and he was stuck there, dangling above the floor.

Of course Attila saw him. A more sympathetic teacher would have realised that Jim had actually improved a lot since his first miserable attempt at this exercise. Attila only saw Jim as a nuisance who was holding up everyone else.

'Oh don't just hang there like a strung-up turkey, Doran,' he snapped. 'This isn't a butcher's shop. This is a gym, Jim!'

Jim heard John Callan mutter, 'Gym Jim!' and he knew that would be the new cat-call in the schoolyard at lunchtime. He gritted his teeth and made a super-human effort to reach the next rung but before his right hand could grasp it, his left hand gave up supporting his weight and he fell with a thud to the floor.

'Flopped again,' sighed the Bun impatiently. 'Tarzan's Granny could do better than that.'

Mary Furlong was next in line and of course she swung swiftly and gracefully from rung to rung all the way across.

'Look at Mary,' said Attila. 'Watch how Mary does it.'

'Like Tarzan's Granny,' muttered Jim under his breath. His knees were sore from his fall on the floor and his feelings were hurt even more. He limped unhappily to the end of the line while the rest of his group took their turn.

Attila the Bun climbed up on the disused vaulting horse and blew his whistle. He was about to shout 'Change!' when to his surprise he heard his own voice calling, 'Everyone sit on the floor!'

Every child in the gym sat down immediately and looked at the Bun to see what he wanted next. He stood there in front of them with his mouth open and a frown on his face. Then he recovered himself and shouted, 'On your feet. Change at the double!'

Everyone leaped up and ran to their next position.

'Begin!' called Attila.

'And do it backwards!' added his voice.

Attila spun around to see who had spoken but there was nothing to be seen but a row of coats and clothes. Meanwhile the class was in a state of confusion. Some were standing doing nothing, others were talking. A few were attempting to climb backwards up the climbing frame and one boy was trying to spring backwards onto the vaulting horse.

'Good old Pin,' muttered Jim. 'Keep it up and don't mind your promise.'

Attila was feeling annoyed but he didn't know who to be angry with. 'Line up in your groups,' he barked, 'and no talking!'

Everyone lined up obediently. Attila opened his mouth but before he could give any further orders the voice started again.

'Group One to the climbing frame,' it called. 'Group Two to the door. Group Three sit down. Group Four to the mats.'

Everyone began to run to their places but as soon as they got there the voice spoke again. 'One swap with Three, Three swap with Four, Two swap with One, Four swap with Two...'

Soon the whole class was running back and forward and

up and down the gym, bumping into each other and getting mixed up with each other's groups. Attila stood with his whistle in his hand and his mouth open, too surprised to do anything.

'Hop on one leg, walk on your knees, roll on the ground, stand on your head!' ordered the voice. Before long the gym was a confusion of bodies waving their legs in the air, tripping over each other, rolling about on the floor or just sitting there looking bewildered. It was like gym day in the lunatic asylum and the class was enjoying every minute of it. This was turning out to be the craziest gym lesson they'd had for years.

Attila blew a blast on his whistle that almost burst his ear drums. 'Sit down and don't move unless I tell you,' he shouted.

Everyone sat where they were, panting from their non-stop exercise. Gradually the noise died away. Attila took a deep breath and waited to see if the voice would speak again. Nothing happened. 'Now we are going to practice hand-stands on the horse,' said Attila quietly, trying to sound as normal as possible. He waited again, listening. The class shifted uneasily. There was obviously something wrong with the Bun this morning. The gym was deathly silent.

'Joe and Tony bring the horse to the centre of the room,' continued Attila.

The boys began to do as they were told.

'Paul Garland and John Callan fetch me the mats.'

Paul and John stood up to obey.

'Mary, go and get me...'

'...a cup of tea and a bun!' shouted the voice.

The class exploded in laughter and Mary stood frozen, not knowing whether to go and get his flask or not.

Attila was enraged. He glared at the class and shouted,

'Who said that?'

'You did, sir,' replied John Callan.

'I did not!' retorted the Bun.

'Oh yes, you did,' chorused a group from the floor. This was getting like a pantomime.

Attila almost said, 'Oh no, I didn't,' but he stopped himself on time. 'Two lines on either side of the vaulting horse!' he shouted, trying desperately to take control of the situation.

The class scrambled to their feet and lined up as they were told. Attila demonstrated the run up to the horse, the spring, the head-stand that changed smoothly into a forward roll and the light drop to the floor.

'Paul Garland, Tony Ryan and Mary Furlong,' he called.

The three children lined up before the horse. At a signal from Attila, Paul ran forward and sprang onto the horse but couldn't hold the handstand. Attila caught him as he over-balanced but he didn't criticise him.

'Now Tony,' called Attila. This was more like it. The lesson was settling down again and he was in command. Tony managed the handstand but his forward roll did not bring him off the horse. He was left sitting on it with his legs on either side.

'You're not supposed to ride the horse!' chirped Attila. 'We're not playing cowboys. Now Mary.'

Mary Furlong tossed her hair back from her face and ran towards the horse. She sprang gracefully into the air, landed steadily on the horse and moved easily into a perfect hand-stand. Her long fair hair fell across the leather top of the horse while her athletic legs pointed straight at the ceiling. She finished with a faultless forward roll and landed easily on the floor.

Attila's eyes were shining with admiration. 'Beautiful. Absolutely perfect,' he purred. 'Please do it again.'

Mary flashed a brilliant smile at the Bun and returned to the starting position. She was about to repeat her perform- ance when Attila's voice said, 'Now watch how Mary does it. I really fancy her!'

'Oooh!' gasped the class and several of them sniggered. Mary Furlong turned bright crimson and hid her face in her hands.

'Who said...?' began the astounded Attila. Then he stopped, confused. Was it possible that he could have said those words out loud? He wasn't sure, for indeed that was what he had been thinking. Sweat broke out all over his face and he stared wild-eyed around the class. Some of them were gazing at him in amazement, others were rolling around the floor in fits of laughter. Mary Furlong began to cry.

'I did not say that!' shouted Attila angrily.

'Oh yes you did,' chorused the children.

'No I did not!' raged the Bun.

'Oh yes you did,' answered the quiet voice of Miss Lynch, who had come to collect her class. 'I heard you myself.'

Attila turned pale.

'I think you'd better go,' said Miss Lynch.

Attila grabbed his coat and the bag that held his flask and his bun, and stormed out of the gym.

That was the last the children ever saw of him.

10   Cat-Calls

All the talk on the way home from school was of Masher Moran's madness and Attila's crazy gym lesson. Children pranced around the pavement imitating Attila's voice and ordering each other to perform ridiculous exercises.

'John, swing like a monkey from that tree!'

'Joe, help Tarzan's granny across the road!'

'Laura, do a handstand on that baby's pram!'

'Jim, do a triple bottom-bouncing turkey flop!'

'No, no. You flopped all wrong. Watch how Mary does it!'

'I really fancy her!'

They fell around the street laughing as they remembered the look of wild confusion on the Bun's face when Miss Lynch said, 'Oh yes you did.'

Caitríona enjoyed the jokes but she said very little. She was busy watching Jim and adding to the plan she had worked out the night before. She noticed that Jim wasn't joining in the fun. She knew he ought to have been, for Masher Moran was his number one enemy in the class and Attila the Bun had made all his Mondays a misery. It all fitted neatly into her plan. Before the night was out she would be sure her guess was correct.

Dinner-time around the Doran's kitchen table was an unusually agreeable affair. Jim was in good humour and for once Caitríona didn't cause any rows by picking on him. Tom and Mary Doran actually managed to get through the meal without having to lose their tempers with anyone.

Jim had been expecting Caitríona to tell the story of Masher and Attila to everyone but to his relief she said nothing at all. The conversation was mostly about the unsuccessful burglary attempt and whether they should install a burglar alarm.

After dinner Eileen washed the dishes and Jim and Caitríona dried them. This was another time when there was usually bickering and bad temper but this evening there was a strange calmness at the sink. Eileen sang her favourite pop songs and Caitríona hummed along with a look of smug satisfaction on her face that made Jim feel uneasy.

Afterwards Caitríona went to her room and stretched herself out on her bed with a sigh of contentment. Her plan to test Jim secretly had worked perfectly. Any normal brother who had been told about the mystery of the jigsaw, the rubic cube, the music box and the mechanical bird, would immediately have told everyone else in the house. Jim had obviously told no one. Why not? Because he didn't want to draw attention to the activities of Pin. And why had he said nothing about the most extraordinary morning they had ever had since they went to school, unless he had something to hide? Caitríona felt sure that Pin was mixed up in that too, though she didn't know how. She decided that the time had come to challenge Jim with her evidence and demand to see the little man.

Jim was sitting at his desk finishing his homework when Caitríona walked right in without knocking. Pin, who had been sitting on the bookshelf in front of him, vanished speedily between two books as soon as the doorhandle rattled.

Caitríona closed the door behind her: then she sat on the end of Jim's bed and said, 'All right. I believe you.'

Jim stared at her. Sometimes the things Caitríona said meant nothing to him because they were downright silly. At other times her brain was three steps ahead of his. He had learned to be cautious and not let her know when he didn't understand her.

'Really?' he said, hoping she might say more and make herself clear.

'Yes,' replied Caitríona. 'I've decided that it wasn't you that stole my chocolates and interfered with the things in my room. You wouldn't have had the time or the patience to complete my jigsaw. You certainly haven't the brains to solve the rubic cube and there's no way you could have fixed the bird or the music box.'

Caitríona paused and looked at him. Jim still felt unsure of himself. Was this just a friendly visit to tell him she wasn't blaming him?

'You're quite right,' he agreed. 'I didn't do any of those things.'

'I know,' replied Caitríona, 'and I've decided that you haven't been talking to the vacuum cleaner or to your slippers, so you're not going mad.'

'Well, thank you very much,' said Jim. 'It's a great relief to know I'm still sane.'

Caitríona looked coolly at him and smiled slightly. 'In fact,' she went on, 'I think you were telling me the truth on

Saturday morning and I believe you.'

With a shock of horror Jim realised what it was that she believed and his heart began to thump.

'What truth?' he asked, though he knew only too well what was coming next.

'The truth about your little man — Pinbidim — or whatever you call him,' she replied. 'I believe you were telling the truth — unlikely as it may seem.'

Jim felt a deep sinking feeling, a sadness as if something precious had been lost. Would he never be able to have anything that was his alone, that nobody else knew about? Up to now, all his life had been open to other people's eyes. His parents oversaw every bite he ate, every article of clothing he wore. On occasions Eileen filled in as a second, though inattentive mother. Cat especially always seemed to be at his side. They had toddled together, been let out to play together, shared their first day in school together. They had always been in the same class. Every incident in school was known to her. If he chose to relate a school story to his parents at the dinner table, Cat was at his elbow correcting him, robbing his jokes of humour, defending his enemies, puncturing his exaggerations, making little of his rare triumphs, magnifying his small defeats. She never let him away with anything. Of course he did the same to her, putting her down instinctively. He couldn't let her glorify herself at his expense. Being with Cat was like living on a see-saw: to push yourself up you had to force the other one down.

Now he looked at Caitríona's alert face and her eyes eager with curiosity and he decided it was a total nuisance having an intelligent sister. For once in his life something really extraordinary had happened to him and it was all his own and nobody else's. Just this once he wanted to hold a real secret to himself, to let nobody know. He was prepared to defend it fiercely against all prying eyes.

He looked coldly at Caitríona and put on what he hoped was a look of superior intelligence.

'You're not serious, Cat, are you?' he drawled, trying to keep his voice cool and sarcastic.

'I am,' she replied, looking steadily into his face.

'Do you mean to say you really believed all that stuff about a little man? I just said that to put you off. At your age you should have given up believing in fairy tales. Really, I thought you were more intelligent than that! Now I see you're just a silly nosy girl.'

Jim hadn't intended to be so spiteful but as he was speaking, more and more nastiness had leaked into his words from somewhere inside his mind.

Caitríona didn't lose her temper. She didn't even reply. Her face sort of crumpled, then she got up, turned quietly away and left the room.

When Jim saw the look of hurt on his sister's face he hated himself for being so cruel, but it was too late. As Caitríona closed the door, Pin emerged from his hiding place and sat with his legs dangling from the bookshelf.

'That wasn't very nice,' he murmured.

Jim looked at him sourly. Pin was right of course but that only made him angrier. 'Who's fault is it that I have to lie to her?' he retorted. 'Who finished her jigsaw, solved her rubic cube and mended her bird?'

Pin glared at him with a face like thunder. Then the cloud of anger passed and his face softened. 'All right,' he agreed, raising his hand in a sign of peace. 'I'm the one who caused all the trouble, as usual. But you got your teeth into her and I'm afraid you enjoyed your bit of nastiness.'

Jim was stung by the truth of what Pin said. 'I was surprised by that myself,' he admitted.

'Good!' breathed Pin. 'We'll have to find a way of undoing that damage. I know you say you hate Caitríona and the pair of you are always snapping at each other, but I can see you are really quite fond of her beneath all the teasing and insults.'

'Don't be silly,' muttered Jim.

'It's true,' insisted Pin. 'What's more, Caitríona is really quite fond of you. You're her only brother. She's closer to you than to Eileen. The struggle between you is a sign of interest. She's curious about you — you're a different creature. She wants to understand you. She'd really like to be friendly but whenever the two of you draw closer together, you clash and drive each other apart.'

Jim stared at his friend. This sudden insight into himself made him feel uncomfortable. 'It's not me she's curious about, it's you, and if she can convince anyone else that you exist then you are in real trouble. You've been too long away from your people, Pin. Your brain is going soft.'

Caitríona wasn't feeling particularly fond of her brother just then. She was lying on her bed, staring at the ceiling and she was furious. She was particularly angry with herself. How could she have been so stupid? It now seemed silly to have believed Jim's story. Even if Jim had a little man he certainly wouldn't have admitted that to her. Why on earth had she walked right in there and announced her foolishness to him? Now he'd be able to taunt her for weeks on end. 'Seen any elves recently Cat?' Everything that happened in the house would be ammunition for his silly jokes. If she complained about the mess he usually left on the kitchen table, he'd say it was Pin who did it. If a pen, or money or a sweet went missing, he'd say, 'Maybe Pin took it.' She hated herself for giving him an advantage over her. She usually had the advantage over him.

She got up and stood glaring at her reflection in the mirror. Then she picked up the metal bird and held it so that its green glass eyes glistened like precious stones in the light. 'If only you could talk,' she sighed as she turned the key and released the bird. She watched it walking and cheeping and pecking. Then she picked it up before it could do its ridiculous back-flip and leg-waving act. The clockwork whirred beneath her fingers. 'One thing I'm certain of,' she declared to the bird. 'Someone fixed you.'

Over by the window the three-thousand-piece jigsaw of Bunratty still lay completed and the perfectly-sided rubic cube on her bookshelf still mocked her inability to solve it herself. Beyond the bedroom wall she could hear the murmur of Jim's voice talking to himself — or to someone else. A sudden rush of frustration made her teeth itch. She turned and kicked her bed.

'Stuff you Jim!' she growled. 'I'm not stupid! There is something going on and you're at the centre of it. You can jeer as much as you like but I'm going to find you out if it kills me.'

❧

Jim didn't jeer Caitríona. In fact he said nothing at all about what had happened between them. As they trudged off to school the following morning she stole a sideways glance at his face and decided he looked gloomy, though whether he was sad or sulky she couldn't tell.

The happenings of the day before were still the main subject of conversation in the school. Masher Moran wasn't in class but no one knew what had become of him. If the children were hoping for more unusual entertainment they were disappointed. They had an ordinary morning's unin-terrrupted work.

Jim was glad of the calm routine. He felt he'd had enough excitement for a while and he still felt unhappy about his conversation with Cat the night before. Pin had decided that he'd rather stay at home than be stuck in Jim's pocket all day and Jim was just as happy not to have him to worry about.

During the mid-morning break Jim joined in a game of football that was all the more enjoyable because Masher Moran wasn't there to jeer his efforts. Caitríona and her friend Laura O'Toole sat on a bench at the gable end of the school watching them.

'Can you keep a secret?' asked Laura as she offered Caitríona a Malteser.

'Of course,' replied Caitríona. 'You can trust me.'

'You know my sister Orla who was going out with Brian Dawney?' whispered Laura.

Caitríona nodded.

'Well, she asked me not to tell anyone, but...' And Laura entertained Caitríona with a juicy tale of how Orla had seen Brian in the town on Saturday afternoon holding another girl's hand and when he came to the house on Sunday they'd had a fantastic row and Orla had been crying in her room and her Dad said she ought to have more sense and then Brian turned up last night with a huge bunch of flowers and said he was sorry and he was even crying...

Caitríona enjoyed the cosiness of sharing Laura's romantic secret as well as the Maltesers and somehow she felt she should share a secret with her friend in return. It would show that she too had something interesting to say and it would draw them closer together and make them special friends. It would also keep her a step ahead of Cissy Sullivan and Mary

Furlong who were always trying to keep Laura to themselves. Besides, the whole business of Jim and Pin had been bubbling up inside her and she felt she would burst if she didn't tell it all to someone. That, at least was what she told herself as she related the whole story to Laura O'Toole.

Laura said nothing for a while. She eyed Caitríona doubtfully. 'You're not having me on, are you?' she asked.

'Of course not!' exclaimed Caitríona. 'Why would I do that?'

'Have you actually seen this little Pin person?' Laura persisted.

'Well, not exactly,' replied Caitríona uneasily. To her disappointment the very act of telling the story had made it seem even more unlikely and she was already beginning to wonder if she had done the right thing. 'You swear you won't tell anyone else?' she asked anxiously.

'Of course I won't,' Laura assured her. 'You know me.'

Then the bell rang and they had to go inside.

Jim was about to sit down when Laura passed behind him.

'Be careful you don't sit on your Pin, Jim,' she said as she went by.

Jim looked quickly at the chair, expecting to see a sneaky drawing pin awaiting his bottom but there was nothing there.

He looked after Laura and as she reached the table she shared with Mary Furlong, she turned and gave Jim a knowing wink. He glanced across at Caitríona and found her staring at him with a worried look on her face. Surely she couldn't have said anything?

'What did Laura mean by that?' asked Pat Duffy as he settled into his place beside Jim.

'I really wish I knew,' Jim sighed as he sat down.

Caitríona knew that her friend had said something. She looked over to the table where Laura and Mary had their heads together in earnest conversation and her worry increased. Why, oh why, had she told Laura everything? When both Laura and Mary turned and grinned at her she was certain her secret was betrayed. Then Mary Furlong passed a note to Cissy Sullivan and Caitríona felt like crying.

'Are you all right, Caitríona?' asked Deirdre Nolan.

Caitríona looked at the girl beside her. She had wispy red hair, pale white skin and large blotchy freckles. Deirdre wasn't very bright. In spite of Miss Lynch's best efforts, Deirdre's silly answers often set the rest of the class laughing at her. In the schoolyard most of the girls ignored her. She tended to hang around on the edge of groups, never managing to belong to anyone. While Caitríona didn't particularly dislike her, she thought her a bit boring and she wasn't pleased that she had to sit beside her.

'Are you all right?' repeated Deirdre.

'Yes, well no,' replied Caitríona. 'I think I've just made a complete fool of myself.'

'Welcome to the club,' murmured Deirdre. 'I do it every day.'

Caitríona looked at the girl beside her and for the first time she began to realise how lonely Deirdre must feel.

'Thanks,' she whispered.

Miss Lynch called the class to order and they were busy with a geography project until the lunch break.

Caitríona didn't want to face the teasing of the other children in the schoolyard, so she waited until most of them had gone out and then asked Miss Lynch if she could stay inside as she wasn't feeling very well.

Miss Lynch, however, had a quick eye for fake illness and Caitríona looked quite healthy to her. 'I think a little walk in the fresh air might do you good,' she said. Then noticing the look on Caitríona's face she added, 'You're not in some sort of trouble, are you?'

Caitríona knew there was no way she could even begin to explain the mess she had landed herself in. 'No Miss,' she replied.

'Well then, off you go,' said Miss Lynch.

Caitríona delayed in the toilets for as long as she could on her way out. By the time she emerged into the noise and bustle of the school yard, every girl in the class had heard the story and some of the boys knew it too. She could tell from the way they turned and looked at her that they were enjoying having her on the menu of their conversations. She decided to ignore them and looked around for Laura but she was nowhere to be seen. 'Hiding from me, no doubt,' muttered Caitríona. As she made her way round to the back of the school, she had to pass a group playing skipping at the corner.

'Here comes the Queen of the Leprechauns!' shouted Cissy Sullivan. 'Does he grant wishes if you catch him?'

Caitríona looked Cissy in the eye. 'If he did, you'd look like the toad you really are!' she retorted.

'Ooh, we really are touchy,' smirked Cissy.

'I heard you had a new Pin-up, boy,' remarked Mary Furlong. 'Couldn't you get someone your own size?'

'Like yourself and the Bun, I suppose,' replied Caitríona sharply.

Mary blushed and said no more.

Caitríona was more than a match for any of them when it came to word battles but she really hated being the one singled out for jeering. As she walked away from them across the wide open space of the yard, she heard their mumbled talk behind her and someone tittering. The back of her neck felt tight and the backs of her legs were wobbly.

'Don't let them bother you.'

Caitríona looked up in surprise. Deirdre Nolan had left the group on the corner and was walking beside her. 'Oh, hi,' replied Caitríona, genuinely glad of Deirdre's company.

'They'll find someone else to make fun of tomorrow,' added Deirdre.

Caitríona thought of all the times she had joined in the laughter against Deirdre. 'We've all done it to you often enough,' she admitted. 'I'm sorry about that.'

'Don't worry about it,' said Deirdre. 'It's often my own fault.'

'And this is definitely mine!' sighed Caitríona, as she spotted a group of her 'friends' over by the basketball court. They seemed to be having an argument with someone. When Caitríona and Deirdre came up behind the group they heard Jim speaking angrily.

Jim had been enjoying a game of four-man tug-o-war using John Callan's school scarf. Pat Duffy and himself had just dragged John Callan and Tony Ryan over one of the lines on the basketball court and were about to win the second round when the girls arrived. The fact that he had even been asked to take part in the game was important to Jim and he wasn't at all pleased to be interrupted by a gang of giggling girls.

When they started quizzing him about Pin, he was horrified. It wasn't long before he realised that they didn't really believe in Pin. They were just trying to make trouble for Caitríona. Knowing that Caitríona was right made it all the more annoying for him to have to deny the story. Even though he was furious with his sister, he didn't want to give ammunition to her enemies. At first he told them to 'Go away and have sense.' But the questions kept on coming.

'Is he a leprechaun?'

'Has he got a pot of gold?'

'Did you catch him in a jam jar at the end of a rainbow?'

The jeering tone of the questions was irritating. He decided to reply in the same style.

'Well,' he said. 'It's partly true. I have a little man, but he's not a leprechaun. He's a Dominillo. In fact I have two dozen of them. I breed them in the back garden under the cabbage leaves. Satisfied?'

'And I suppose they all have magic powers?' smirked Andrea Smith.

'Of course,' replied Jim. 'That's how we got rid of Masher and the Bun.'

The questioners looked at each other, unsure for a second if he might not be telling some kind of truth.

'Could Pin fix my bike?' asked John Callan, giving Jim a broad wink to show he understood the game.

'I wish he could fix their brains,' said Jim sarcastically. 'Look girls, will you all just leave me alone. Go and ask Caitríona what she means. I'm not responsible for her ravings.'

He'd no sooner said it than he was sorry. Now they'd go and tell her that he'd said she was raving mad.

Caitríona and Deirdre had been standing unnoticed at the back of the group. They moved quickly away and headed back towards the school. Behind them the question session had turned into a jeering match between the boys and the girls.

'I thought Laura would have been with that lot,' muttered Caitríona angrily.

'I don't think she came outside at all,' said Deirdre. 'She probably doesn't want to meet you.'

'Well I want to meet her,' growled Caitríona.

They passed the skipping group again. The girls who were waiting their turn were chanting a rhyme that showed only too clearly how fully Laura had betrayed Caitríona's secret.

'Jim in the garden putting out the bin,
Took off the lid and there was Pin.
Pin in the bathroom,
Pin on the street,
Pin in the bedroom,
Stealing Cat's sweet!'

Caitríona was raging but before she could say anything the bell rang and everyone ran to their line. Caitríona followed slowly, watching out for Laura. She was almost at the line when she saw her lurking on the corridor inside the main door. She was obviously hoping to join the class as they came in. Ignoring the school rule about lining up, Caitríona headed for the door and took Laura by surprise. She caught her by the sleeve of her cardigan as Laura tried to escape.

'Blabbermouth!' shouted Caitríona. 'I thought you were my friend.'

'I was — I mean — I am!' stammered Laura. 'It just sort of slipped out.'

'Slipped out!' exploded Caitríona. 'It didn't take long to slip!'

'Well, it was a silly story anyway,' retorted Laura resentfully. 'You hardly expected me to believe it, did you?'

'Even if you didn't, you shouldn't have passed it around to everyone else,' replied Caitríona. 'It was our secret and you promised not to tell. Anyway, do you really think I'd make up something as unlikely as that?'

Laura considered this for a second. 'I don't know really. I didn't think...'

'That's the truest thing you've said today,' snapped Caitríona. 'You didn't think.'

Then they heard the main door opening and Miss Lynch reminding the class to wipe their feet as they came in. The two girls turned and ran down the corridor to their classroom hoping the teacher wouldn't notice they were in ahead of the others.

The rest of the afternoon passed quietly enough except for an incident during the English lesson. Miss Lynch decided to read a poem to the class. Unfortunately the opening verse was:

'Up the airy mountain,
Down the rushy glen,
We daren't go a-hunting
For fear of little men.'

A titter ran around the classroom and everyone turned to look at either Jim or Caitríona. Jim groaned and Caitríona blushed and scowled.

'What's so funny about that?' asked the puzzled Miss Lynch.

No one was willing to try to explain and the class settled down again until the final bell rang.

11 Caitríona Strikes Back

Jim and Caitríona had an uncomfortable walk home from school. They had to put up with quite a lot of not very clever remarks and cat-calls.

'Hey Jim! Could Pin do my homework for me?'

'Watch out for goblins Caitríona!'

'Is he a drawing Pin or a safety Pin?'

By the time they reached their front door they were both completely fed up. They hadn't spoken to each other all the way home but as Jim took out his door key he looked glumly at his sister and said, 'Are you satisfied now?'

'No I'm not!' snapped Caitríona and she pushed past him and ran upstairs to her room.

When he'd said hello to his Mam, Jim went to his own room. Pin was sitting on the desk, hidden behind an atlas he was reading. Jim dropped his bag on the floor and flopped onto the bed. 'Good evening Pin,' he said heavily.

The broad hat and a pair of twinkling eyes appeared above the edge of the atlas.

'Good evening Jim,' returned Pin. 'Did you have a good day at school?'

'Good is not the word I'd use to describe it,' sighed Jim.

'Ah!' breathed Pin, slightly lowering his atlas. 'Perhaps I can distract you from your gloomy thoughts with a little geography. Do you know where Pindiga is?'

'Never heard of it,' replied Jim.

'It's in Nigeria,' said Pin. 'How about Pinega?'

'How about it?' echoed Jim.

'That's a river in Russia,' said Pin.

'How interesting!' gasped Jim, though it was clear he wasn't interested at all.

'Do you know where Pinerolo is?' persisted Pin.

'Let me guess,' said Jim. 'It sounds Italian.'

'Very good!' exclaimed Pin. 'What about Pinkiang?'

'That has to be in China,' replied Jim.

'Well done, you're improving,' said Pin. 'Now try Pinnaroo.'

'Pin my friend,' sighed Jim. 'Could it be that your learned interest in these places has something to do with the fact that your name is in every one of them?'

'Of course,' replied Pin. 'It shows that I'm world famous. Do you know of anywhere that has Jim in its name?'

'None that I can think of,' admitted Jim.

'Perhaps you should read your atlas more often,' smiled Pin. 'Oh, and Pinnaroo is in Australia.'

'Now I've got a question for you,' said Jim. 'Do you know where Pin-mania is?'

'Pin-mania? I don't think that's in this atlas,' said Pin.

'No, it's not in the atlas,' agreed Jim, 'but it's all over our school.'

'What are you talking about?' asked Pin.

'I'm talking about a heap of trouble that Cat caused in school today,' answered Jim and he told the whole story to his friend. By the time he was finished, his mother was calling him down for dinner.

'Chew on that while you're waiting for some food,' said Jim as he heaved himself off the bed and headed for the door.

'I've got indigestion already,' grumbled Pin.

Neither Jim nor Caitríona said very much at the table that evening. Caitríona was waiting for Jim to tell everyone how she'd made a complete fool of herself in school but he didn't even mention it. Once again his silence told her that she couldn't be entirely wrong. He usually enjoyed relating her mistakes.

Tom Doran couldn't believe his good luck in having two peaceful dinners in a row. Mary Doran noticed that Caitríona wasn't eating very much and she wondered if she might be sick.

'Are you sure you're feeling all right, Caitríona?' she asked anxiously. 'You're very quiet this evening.'

'Don't complain about it,' advised her husband. 'It only happens once every six months. Just enjoy it while it lasts!'

After dinner Jim sneaked Pin's meal up to him. He'd managed to gather some chopped apple, celery and sultanas along with a cube of cheese and a savoury biscuit. While Pin was eating, Jim tried to finish his homework but his mind was filled with the doings of the day rather than the events of history and he kept making silly mistakes. When he discovered he had written 'the Vikings set sail in their Laura boats', he threw his pen on the table and turned to Pin.

'What am I going to do about her?' he asked.

'Caitríona?'

'Who else?'

Pin looked thoughtfully at him. 'Tell her the truth and let her see me,' he said.

'You can't be serious!' exclaimed Jim in horror.

'Of course I am,' replied Pin.

'What good would that do?' objected Jim.

'It would satisfy her curiosity,' said Pin, 'and it would restore her self-confidence by answering all the questions that are buzzing around like wasps inside her head. She'll be so pleased to actually see me that her anger will be scattered like a morning mist in a dawn wind. A happy Caitríona will be a lot less trouble.'

'You don't know my sister,' said Jim. 'There's no such thing as a happy Caitríona. Besides, if we let her see you she'll want to show you to everyone to prove that she wasn't making up silly stories.'

'Maybe,' murmured Pin. 'But I think we could persuade her that it wasn't necessary to do that. In my opinion she's even more dangerous as she is.'

Jim picked up his pen and got on with his homework. Obviously Pin didn't know very much about sisters.

At bedtime, Jim's dangerous sister picked up the jigsaw and flung it into its box, taking care to break up every part of it before she put the box away with her other jigsaws. Next she took the rubic cube and savagely twisted it, as if it was someone's neck. When the puzzle was totally undone, she got into bed and switched off her bedside light.

She lay there staring into the half-darkness, waiting for sleep but her angry brain was fully switched on and churning like a washing machine. She decided to clear her mind of everything that had upset her during the day and for a while she succeeded. Her thoughts wandered among the dim shadows of her room. Sounds drifted in from the night street: footsteps approaching, passing, fading; voices murmuring, then suddenly laughing too loud in the stillness. She hated being laughed at. They all thought she was silly, believing in fairies at her age. She'd kill that Laura. She'd love to come from behind and kick her. She was so annoyed she could bite her arm ...

Caitríona shifted on her bed. A line of yellow light glowed under her bedroom door. She heard Eileen's footsteps passing into her bedroom and the click of the light switch. She wished she was grown-up like Eileen, beyond being laughed at.

She could hear Jim mumbling behind the wall. He was always muttering to himself. When he thought no one was listening he staged fights with imaginary enemies, making all the sounds of blows falling, explosions, groans of agony, cries of anger. Jim was a real idiot most of the time. Nearly all the other girls had brothers who were idiots too. Maybe being an idiot was normal for boys. They probably grew out of it in their twenties, unless they turned into PE teachers like the Bun. Jim had told the girls his 'leprechaun' had got rid of the Bun. Jim often said things as a joke that were really true, or half-true at least. He must have had Pin with him in school! If only she'd known! They wouldn't have been laughing at her then. She could have told them to look in Jim's pocket. To think he stood there with Pin in his pocket and told them all that she was raving! The dirty, sneaky liar of a brother ...

She recognised the sound of the Late News on television downstairs and realised she'd been lying there thinking for more than two hours. This was ridiculous. She really must get to sleep or she'd be wrecked in the morning. Maybe her Mam would let her stay off school if she looked tired enough.

She didn't want to face that sniggering shower of sillies, whispering behind her back, shouting stupid Pin-things at her. They were so dull they couldn't even jeer properly.

The television was switched off. She heard her parents locking the front door, then treading heavily on the stairs.

She felt a sudden mad urge to leap out of bed, fling her door open and announce to their startled faces, 'Jim has a little man in his bedroom who fixes things!' It would be such a relief to do it. They would think she was crazy, of course.

She listened to her parents' familiar movements until the line of light below her door vanished and the house fell silent at last. Caitríona twisted and turned in her bed, arguing with herself, reliving the annoyances of the day, taking imaginary revenge on her enemies, guessing at what they might say to her tomorrow and trying to think of clever replies she could make. If only she could prove she was right. If only she could be completely sure herself ...

It must have been about half-past one in the morning when she gave up trying to sleep and decided to go downstairs and comfort herself with a secret snack. It would be a lot better than rolling about in bed. She got up, put on her dressing gown and slippers and crept softly to the door. She gripped the handle firmly and gently pressed it down, then she drew the door towards herself. It opened without a squeak. Slowly she moved the handle upwards again and released it. Then she paused and listened. In the silence she could hear the steady breathing of her parents in their bedroom. They always slept with their door open so they could hear if any of the children were disturbed.

Caitríona looked out from her room, trying to gather the courage to step onto the landing and steal downstairs alone. A pale shaft of moonlight slanted from the window at the turn of the stairs, casting a ghostly light on the carpet.

Suddenly, every nerve in Caitríona's body leaped and she almost cried out in fear. In the silvery light, halfway down the stairs, sat the figure of a tiny man! His face was hidden by a broad hat but she could clearly see his little hands resting on the step where he was sitting. Caitríona's heart was thundering inside her and her legs trembled so much she wished she could sit down. It must be Pin! Pin before her very eyes!

The next instant he slid off the step as swift as a squirrel and vanished down the stairs. Had she really seen him? Of course she had!

She mustn't let him get away. She moved quickly to the top step and looked over the banisters. He had paused for a moment at the bottom of the stairs. To her amazement, he did two cartwheels across the carpet. After that he did a hand-stand and walked in a circle on his hands. Then he sprang to his feet like an olympic gymnast and swaggered down the hall singing happily to himself.

'He's marvellous!' whispered Caitríona. Now everyone would know she was right. Caitríona Doran did not make up silly childish stories. She would show them and Jim would have to admit it. Raving indeed!

She took two steps down the stairs, then stopped. What was she going to do? Catch him and keep him prisoner until she could bring him to school and show the others? Would she be able to catch him? Would she be able to tie him up? Even if she was able, she wasn't sure she really wanted to. Suppose he was magic? He might put a spell on her if she treated him badly. Oh, what was she to do? It would be no good just to tell the others that she'd actually seen him dancing in the moonlight in the middle of the night. They'd be even more sure she was a silly liar. There had to be some way of proving it.

As if by real magic a marvellous idea flashed into her mind.

'Caitríona, you're a genius!' she whispered as she hurried to her room and took her new camera from her drawer. She adjusted the setting to flash and made sure the film was wound on. Then she tip-toed out of her room and stole quickly down the stairs. She paused in the hall and listened. From the kitchen came the faint sound of singing, then she heard the familiar rattle of the biscuit barrel. Of course, Pin was the mysterious biscuit-thief.

Caitríona's heart was thumping again. She must be quick and she must be deadly accurate. Like a big game hunter shooting at a charging tiger, there would be no second chance if she missed the first time. She checked the camera again, then dizzy with fear and excitement she stepped into the kitchen.

It all happened in less than five seconds. With a single glance Caitríona's eyes took in the kitchen, lit by the pale moon-glow. She saw the dim figure of Pin on the worktop beside the biscuit barrel and caught the sudden upward jerk of his head as he saw her. Swiftly her camera was raised, her finger pressed and light exploded from the flash. The biscuit barrel rolled across the worktop and crashed to the floor. She was aware of a scurry of movement down the front of the clothes horse but she flicked the film forward and flashed again like a hunter determined to kill her fleeing prey. Pin escaped into the hallway at an amazing speed. Caitríona fired again. Then it was over. Pin was gone.

Caitríona stood alone in the kitchen and discovered to her surprise that she was out of breath. Her first feeling was one of loss. Pin was gone and she hadn't really met him. They hadn't spoken or even looked at each other in any normal kind of way. The whole thing had been an attack.

She had expected to feel excited and victorious. All she felt was disappointment and a great heavy-headed weariness.

The undeveloped polaroid photos were in her left hand. She couldn't even remember taking them from the camera. She slid them into her pocket.

She struggled up the stairs again, not even trying to look out for Pin. When she got to her room she put the photos on her dressing table and peeled off the paper covers. In a few moments the pictures would be ready. She sat on the edge of the bed, then without bothering to take off her dressing-gown, she slid gratefully beneath her duvet. She was surprised to find the bed still warm and she let her weight sink into the welcoming mattress. Still clutching her precious camera, Caitríona closed her eyes and was immediately asleep.

❧

Caitríona wondered who could be banging a drum in the house first thing in the morning. Then she realised that someone was pounding on her door.

'Get up, sleepy-head!' shouted Eileen. 'It's the end of the world and if you don't hurry you'll miss it!'

'Very funny,' moaned Caitríona as she struggled up from under her duvet and suddenly realised she had the camera in bed with her. Then she remembered the night before. It was almost like a dream: lying awake for hours; Pin sitting in the moonlight, sliding down the stairs, dancing in the hall; the photographic attack in the kitchen. She stared at the camera. Supposing it really was a dream, just something let loose by her exhausted imagination? Well, there was one way to prove it. The photos were lying on her dressing table. If it was true, Pin would be captured there on film. If it was a dream, she would have three shiny black rectangles.

She got out of bed and slid her feet into her slippers. From the kitchen she could hear Jim and Eileen talking, then her mother's voice telling them to get on with their breakfasts. Her father would be already on his way to work.

With a feeling close to dread, she stepped over to the dressing table and looked at the photos. The first one had caught Pin in the act of stealing a chocolate biscuit. It was as good a shot as Caitríona could have wished for. Pin's face was clearly visible and he looked most surprised indeed. He was holding the biscuit in both his hands and had just taken a bite from it. Caitríona giggled at the expression on his face. He looked just like a naughty child who has been caught in the act by an angry parent.

The second shot showed Pin scrambling down the clothes horse and the last shot had caught him in the doorway of the hall. He had his back to the camera and one leg was raised as he ran. He looked tiny framed by the doorway. He had turned his head to glance back at her as he fled and the camera had caught the fear in his eye.

'Now, I've got you!' murmured Caitríona. She carefully placed the photos in her dressing table drawer and hurried down to breakfast.

Eileen left the kitchen as Caitríona came in. Mrs Doran had just finished making the children's lunches. 'You're a slow-coach this morning, Caitríona,' she remarked.

'Yes,' admitted Caitríona. 'I didn't really get much sleep last night.' She looked meaningfully at Jim who was finishing a bowl of cereal but he kept his eyes on his food.

'Well, don't dawdle over your breakfast or you'll be late for school,' advised Mrs Doran as she left the kitchen.

Caitríona filled herself a bowl of cornflakes and sliced a banana into it. She sat at the table and began to eat. Jim said nothing. She wondered if he knew what had happened last night. She decided to test him.

'Do you still think I'm "raving"?' she asked.

Jim noisily scraped his bowl, then he pushed back his chair and stood up. He looked coldly at his sister. 'I think you're a bloody nuisance!' he snapped and he strode out of the kitchen.

Caitríona was so annoyed she could scarcely eat her breakfast. She had intended inviting Jim to her room and showing him the photos. Now that seemed much too soft a way to deal with him. 'I'll show you,' she growled to herself. 'I'll make more trouble for you than you could ever imagine. You'll be sorry. They'll all be sorry.'

As Caitríona was passing through the hall after her breakfast, the letter box clattered and the local paper, the *Daily Dawn*, thudded onto the floor. By the time she had reached her room, a daring plan for revenge on her mockers was racing through her mind. This would really take them all by surprise and leave Jim with a lot of questions to answer. It was such a brilliant plan that she laughed out loud and danced around the floor of her bedroom. The very idea of it was so exciting that Caitríona didn't even pause to consider the avalanche of trouble it would pull down on top of everyone.

As soon as she was washed and dressed, she took a writing pad from the drawer of her desk and wrote a short note on a page that was decorated with spring flowers. Then she put the note, along with the photo of Pin in the hall doorway, into a fancy pink envelope and sealed it. She slid the envelope into her anorak pocket, picked up her schoolbag and headed down the stairs.

Jim had already left for school but this suited Caitríona's plan perfectly. She called 'Goodbye' to her Mam and set off with a lively step and a great sense of excitement. She kept well away from any groups of children heading for the school and she was very glad that she didn't meet Laura on the way.

The offices of the *Daily Dawn* were on the first floor above the Hardware and Gardening Centre on Main Street. Having checked that no one was looking, Caitríona stepped in through the doorway and hurried upstairs. The office door was shut but she could hear voices inside and the clack-clack of a typewriter. Going inside would involve difficult explanations and keep her late for school, so she dropped the pink envelope through the letter-box and fled down the stairs, afraid that someone would open the door and call her back.

Once she was out in the sunny street again she breathed a sigh of relief. It was strange how delivering that envelope had made her feel guilty, as if she had committed a crime. Even as she hurried on to school, she couldn't escape the feeling that everyone she passed was looking at her, wondering about her.

The bell was clanging as she reached the school gate. She braced herself to face the jeers and jokes again. Today would be different. Today she was certain she was right. They could mock as much as they liked. She wouldn't even bother to answer them. She would keep a dignified silence, holding her head proudly. Perhaps she might allow a slight mysterious smile to play about her lips as she gazed dreamily into the distance. They would wonder then if she really knew something special. Oh yes, she knew. She even knew something that Jim didn't know.

As the bell stopped ringing, Caitríona walked calmly across the schoolyard to join her class.

Mike Kelly, the editor of the *Daily Dawn*, ripped open the pink envelope and shook the contents onto his desk. He glanced curiously at the photo and wondered what sort of new doll it could be. When he saw the childish handwriting and the flowery paper, he grunted to himself. Then he read the note.

> Dear Sir,
> This is my brother's little man. His name is Pin. He's a genius at fixing things. I'm sending this photo to you to prove he exists because my brother pretends he doesn't and my friends all laugh at me. I took this photo in my kitchen in the middle of the night while Pin was stealing a biscuit.
> Yours truly,
> *Caitríona.*

Mike Kelly was a very busy man with no time for non-sense. Letters from over-imaginative children having dis-agreements with their brothers were a waste of time to him. He tossed the letter aside and got on with his work.

That might have been the end of it but during lunchtime Mike Kelly received a visit from Bob Whaley. 'The Whale' as his American friends called him, was a journalist with the *Boston Bugle*. He was touring Ireland, disturbing his long-lost relatives and he had decided to drop in on the local paper, have a chat with some Irish journalists and get to know the publishing scene in what he called the 'Emerald Isle'.

Mike took out two glasses and the bottle of Jameson Irish Whiskey that he kept under his desk for special visitors and the two men swopped tales of news stories and sympathised with each other over rival newspapers, lazy reporters and unhelpful politicians.

Then Bob's eye fell on Caitríona's photo.

'Hey man!' he exclaimed. 'Is this a genuine Irish leprechaun?'

'Oh it's just some...' began Mike.

But Bob was far too excited to listen to him. He read Caitríona's note aloud, then he held the photo up to the light and his eyes grew wide with wonder. 'Gee!' he gasped. 'I've never seen an actual photo of a real live leprechaun. To tell you the truth, I didn't believe they existed.'

Mike was frowning at him. 'They don't,' he said abruptly, and he put the Jameson bottle under his desk again.

'Well what's this then?' insisted Bob, tapping the photo with a pudgy forefinger.

'A hoax,' grunted Mike.

'If it is, it's a hell of a good one,' insisted Bob. 'The body shape is perfect.'

'It's probably one of those new dolls they bring out every year for the Christmas market,' said Mike.

'That's no doll,' declared Bob. 'That shot has movement. Look at the position of the legs and the turn of the head. He looks like he's running for cover. Look at his startled face. He was definitely taken by surprise and he wasn't too happy about it either. If that's a hoax, then it's a really good one. They thought of all the angles.'

Mike stared at him. Then he took the photo and examined it again. What Bob had said was true. Mike looked at the American's excited face. 'But it was sent in by a little girl,' he objected.

'All the better, man,' insisted Bob. 'It gives a sentimental flavour to the story. Listen, a yarn like this would go down a bomb in the States: "Genuine Irish leprechaun snapped by an innocent Irish coleen." Fantastic!'

'You're not seriously suggesting I should publish it?'

exclaimed Mike.

'Why not?' demanded Bob. 'There's some sort of story behind this, even if it isn't a leprechaun. And I — I mean you — could sell it to the *Boston Bugle* or the *New York Yippee* and make a nice profit.'

'They wouldn't use it,' objected Mike. 'They wouldn't want to make themselves look foolish.'

'No problem,' drawled the Whale, flicking away the difficulty with a wave of his fat hand. 'They don't say it's true. They say "It was reported in the *Daily Dawn* in Ireland that ... etc etc." They publish your story, and your photo and bingo! — your little local paper is quoted in the big international dailies. Next thing you know every advertiser in Ireland is wanting to buy space on your pages and man, you're making dollars hand over fist!'

Mike Kelly was tempted by the idea but he was still not sure. 'Even if you're right, it would only be a flash-in-the-pan. It wouldn't last long enough to make real money.'

'Not at all,' insisted Bob. 'You'd have people from all over Ireland writing to say there were no such things as leprechauns and others claiming that their Uncle Jack once nearly caught one. You'd have letters pouring in from the States from folks who swear they saw one after an all-night party they had with their relatives in Ballygoloony. Gee man, this could run until next year. You might even get the local politicians talking about it and there'd be questions in that Dáil-place of yours.'

Mike laughed. 'I'll say one thing for you, Bob — you've got a great imagination. OK, I'll give it a run. It can't do much harm, I suppose.'

❧

Caitríona told no one what she had done. Jim had expected her to continue insisting that her story was true, but in the face of constant 'Pin' remarks from the other children she remained strangely calm. He was relieved but rather puzzled.

At break time the schoolyard was full of awful leprechaun jokes. Everyone seemed to have one and they all wanted to try them out on Jim and Caitríona.

'Hey Jim,' shouted Joe McGlinn. 'What do you call a leprechaun falling down a hill?'

'I've no idea,' sighed Jim.

'A rolling Pin! Do you get it?'

'I would if there was anything to get,' retorted Jim.

'What do you call a leprechaun sitting on a bald man's head?' shouted Cissy Sullivan.

Caitríona didn't bother to reply.

'A hair-Pin!' giggled Cissy.

'What do you call ten leprechauns playing marbles?' asked John Callan.

Jim shrugged.

'Ten Pin bowling!' laughed John.

'What do you get if you sit on a leprechaun?' asked Paul Garland.

'A year's supply of bad jokes,' muttered Jim.

'No. A Pin-cushion!'

Caitríona walked around with Deirdre Nolan and kept a straight, serious face. This wasn't too difficult as most of the jokes were pathetic. Jim eventually got involved in a game of football and in the excitement of the game he forgot about his trouble until John Callan shouted, 'Come on Pin, shoot!' The others took it up with good-humoured cries of, 'Over here Pin, pass it here.' 'Good shot, Pin!' Jim knew then that he had a new nickname. He didn't really mind too much. It was better than Tinchy.

By the time they were going home, the class had run out of Pin jokes and things had calmed down a little. Caitríona said nothing further to Jim about believing in Pin and Jim began to think he had been wise to ignore Pin's advice about letting Cat see him.

They had a quiet evening at home. Jim spent most of the time playing chess with Pin, who was turning out to be a very crafty player. After supper, as Jim and his sister were heading upstairs, Caitríona paused outside her bedroom, stretched herself dramatically and with a loud sigh said, 'I think tomorrow will be a surprising day!'

Jim was directly behind her on the stairs. He looked at her suspiciously as she disappeared into her room and muttered, 'What next? I've had enough surprises to last me a lifetime.'

He couldn't see Pin when he entered his room.

'Pin!' he called softly.

There was a movement along the closed curtains at the window and Pin appeared like a performer from behind a stage curtain. He greeted Jim with a doubtful smile.

'What on earth were you doing in there?' asked Jim.

'Partly hiding,' replied Pin, 'partly looking at the back garden.'

'There can't be much to see out there at this time of night,' commented Jim.

'Not a lot,' agreed Pin as he walked along the edge of the window-sill and hopped lightly down onto Jim's desk. 'I like looking at the lights in other people's houses. It reminds me of home.'

There was a note of loneliness in Pin's voice that made Jim look carefully at him for a moment.

'Caitríona has been acting strangely today,' Jim remarked, as he got into his pyjamas.

'According to you, she's always strange,' said Pin.

'This is different,' replied Jim. 'She's peculiarly calm and she has just announced that tomorrow will be a surprising day, as if she has arranged the surprise herself.'

Pin shifted uneasily on the pillow. Jim thought the little man had a guilty look on his face.

'Pin?' he asked. 'Are you hiding something from me?'

Pin looked startled. 'What could I possibly be hiding from you?' he murmured.

'If I knew I wouldn't have to ask, would I?' replied Jim.

Pin's face settled into his stubborn look. Jim sighed. He was certain now that Pin had caused some new trouble.

'Look Pin,' he said. 'If I know what the problem is, then I may be able to do something about it.'

Pin's face grew even more stubborn. 'I won't be a problem to you for very much longer,' he replied in a voice full of self-pity.

Jim raised his eyes to the ceiling. 'You know, Pin, there are times when you can be totally impossible!' he growled as he leaned over to switch off the light.

12 The *Daily Dawn*

The following morning Caitríona was as jumpy as a squirrel. She could scarcely eat her cereal and twice during breakfast she leaped up from the table and ran out into the hall. Then she tripped over Matsa on her way back to the table.

'What on earth is the matter with you, child?' asked Mary Doran.

'I thought I heard a noise in the hall,' replied Caitríona.

'What noise could there be in the hall?' said her mother. 'Are you still worrying about the burglars?'

'The noise of her clattering her spoon off that bowl and slurping her milk would scare away any burglars,' complained Eileen, who was always grumpy at breakfast.

Matsa miaowed from under the table as if she agreed.

Caitríona escaped from the kitchen. In the hallway she stared at the letter box but the *Daily Dawn* hadn't been delivered yet. This wasn't unusual. Sometimes it came before she left the house, othertimes after. Up to now she'd never noticed it. This morning she just couldn't wait to get her hands on the paper.

Jim came sleepily down the stairs. 'Got your surprise yet?' he yawned.

'You're the one who'll get the surprise,' snapped Caitríona as she ran up to the bathroom.

'I was afraid of that,' muttered Jim as he headed for the kitchen.

Caitríona hung around the house for as long as she could but the *Daily Dawn* didn't come. In the end her mother had to take her by the arm and push her out the door. Caitríona ran all the way to school to avoid being late. By the time she reached the school gate she was hot and breathless and bursting with frustration. What if someone else had seen the paper and she hadn't? This was the worst possible way to face the class.

No one mentioned it. By the end of the maths lesson Caitríona had calmed down. Then she began to feel disappointed. The stupid *Daily Dawn* hadn't published it. She should have known they wouldn't. All they ever had were boring letters about the traffic and the amount of crime in town and photos of dead people on their anniversaries and grinning grown-ups getting married. They never printed anything exciting.

The Pin jokes had almost dried up and interest in Caitríona's story seemed to be dying down. Miss Lynch kept the class very busy all day and she ended the afternoon by giving them a large homework.

As Caitríona hurried home from school she began to feel nervous again. What if her mother had seen the paper? Would she know who had written the letter? Why hadn't she just told her parents?

By the time she reached her own front door she was so

jumpy she dropped her key twice. Eileen opened the door while she was picking the key up again.

'Are you all right?' asked Eileen.

'Of course I am!' snapped Caitríona as she pushed past her sister into the hall.

'Pardon my asking,' muttered Eileen.

Caitríona ignored her. She was itching to see the paper. She half-hoped there would be nothing in it. It would be easier that way. When she walked into the kitchen she almost collapsed. Her mother was sitting at the table drinking tea and reading the *Daily Dawn*!

'Hello Mam,' Caitríona said shakily.

'Hello dear,' replied her mother. 'How was your day?'

'All right,' answered Caitríona.

'Good,' said Mrs Doran.

That was all. No fuss. No questions. She hadn't seen it, or it wasn't there to be seen. Caitríona delayed over a glass of milk and a biscuit, hoping to get her hands on the wretched paper but her mother was in no hurry — the dinner was roasting in the oven, the ironing was completed and all was right with the house. In the end Caitríona gave up and went upstairs to do her homework.

After dinner, Tom Doran took the paper as he usually did and settled down for a relaxed read while he digested his meal. Caitríona could have screamed. She knew her father could keep the paper for an hour or more if he was in a reading humour.

It was Jim's turn to do the dinner wash-up with Eileen.

Caitríona surprised everyone by volunteering to take his place. Of course she didn't say that she really wanted to stay near to her father so she could snatch up the *Daily Dawn* as soon as he left it down.

Jim was delighted to escape upstairs to Pin. They had been

playing chess and the score was level at two games all. Pin was very crafty but rather impatient. He made his moves quickly and complained if Jim took too long in working out his next move. He also crowed and boasted too much when he won. Tonight Jim was determined to take the lead and show the little big-head that he had a brain as well.

By the time the wash-up was finished Tom Doran had settled into a comfortable armchair in the sittingroom and was working his way through the sports pages. Caitríona was determined not to let the paper out of her sight, so she sat beside her father and tried to pretend she was interested in Eileen's favourite television programme, Fantasy Fashions. She was almost howling with boredom by the time her father decided he wanted to see the Nine O'Clock News. The instant he put the paper down Caitríona snatched it up.

'Don't go messing that up on me,' he warned. 'I'm not finished with it yet.'

'Don't worry,' promised Caitríona as she scurried into the kitchen with it. She spread it out on the table and hurriedly turned the pages. She got to the back page without seeing anything. Half-disappointed and half-relieved she went back to the front page and worked her way through again.

Though Mike Kelly had eventually been persuaded to publish the letter and photo, he had decided to play it safe and not give it too important a place. So when Caitríona at last found the photograph, it wasn't with the other letters to the editor but tucked away on the second last page above a crossword puzzle, under the title 'Now Who Believes in the Little People?' The article read: 'This photo and the accompanying note were handed in to us by a young girl. She actually succeeded in catching the little fellow in the act of stealing a biscuit from her kitchen. If anyone else has seen one of these Little People we would be glad to hear from them.' The print of the photo wasn't great but it was definitely Pin and the surprise was clear on his face. Caitríona's letter was printed below the picture. She wasn't too pleased with this either. A printer's error had changed 'He's a genius at fixing things' into 'He's a genius at mixing things' and they had written Caitríona's name as Catroona!

Obviously neither of her parents had bothered to look at the article. Perhaps nobody would. She decided to wait and see.

✥

The following morning Deirdre Nolan met Caitríona at the school gate. She was wide-eyed with excitement. 'Did you send a letter and a photo of Pin to the *Daily Dawn*?' she asked.

Caitríona felt a leap of fright inside her. 'Yes, I did,' she replied.

'So it really is true!' exclaimed Deirdre.

'Of course it's true,' said Caitríona. 'I thought you believed me.'

'I didn't know what to believe,' replied Deirdre, 'but I knew they shouldn't have made fun of you whether it was true or not.'

Caitríona understood that nobody could have been expected to believe her story. She also realised that Deirdre had behaved like a real friend, for she had remained loyal to Caitríona even when she seemed to be making a fool of herself.

'Has anyone else seen it?' Caitríona asked as they walked across the schoolyard.

'I don't think so,' replied Deirdre. 'No one mentioned it and I didn't say anything about it.'

'Good,' breathed Caitríona. 'Could you keep it as a secret just between us for a while?'

'Of course,' agreed Deirdre, 'but they're bound to find out pretty soon.'

'I know,' admitted Caitríona, 'but I'd rather wait a bit.'

The bell rang and they all went into class. Laura O'Toole was absent until after the mid-morning break. She came in while the others were writing a story and handed a note to Miss Lynch. On her way to her desk she gave Caitríona a broad wink and whispered, 'See you at break time, Catroona!'

Caitríona and Deirdre looked at each other. They knew that Laura would tell everyone.

Laura did more than tell. She showed everyone. When they were out in the yard during lunchbreak she produced the article from her pocket like a magician pulling a rabbit from a hat.

'You crafty thing!' she squeaked excitedly to Caitríona. 'It's absolutely brilliant!'

Soon a crowd was gathered around Laura and Caitríona demanding to see the photo. Laura seemed to have forgotten that she was the one who had first made fun of Caitríona's story. Now she was acting as if she had done something great by finding the photo. If Caitríona was to be the centre of attraction then Laura was going to stay right there with her to share the glory.

Caitríona was beginning to enjoy the attention she was getting but she knew what Laura was doing and she made sure to keep Deirdre beside her all the time.

'Why didn't you tell anyone about the photograph?' asked Mary Furlong with a sulky look on her face.

'Deirdre knew about it,' replied Caitríona, 'but I asked her to say nothing and she kept her word.'

Deirdre smiled, pleased at receiving a rare word of public praise.

There were dozens of questions. It was like being a famous pop-singer or film-star. Most of the questioners were genuinely curious, a few were unfriendly, calling the picture a fake.

'Look,' sighed Caitríona. 'You didn't believe me when I told you about Pin before. Well, there he is. He's really Jim's friend and he knows a lot more about him than I do.'

'Jim said you were raving the last time we asked him,' sneered Cissy Sullivan, who was feeling jealous of all the attention Caitríona was getting, particularly from Laura.

'Go and see what he says now,' retorted Caitríona proudly. Her moment of triumph had come. Her brother would have to admit the truth and treat her fairly in front of the others.

Jim was playing basketball with John Callan, Tony Ryan and Joe McGlinn. He was in good humour because Joe had just told him for certain that Masher Moran was now attending a different school and definitely wouldn't be coming back. His good humour didn't last very long.

John Callan was about to take a penalty shot at the basket when he froze with a look of alarm on his face. 'Somebody is in big trouble,' he murmured.

The others turned and looked. A group of over twenty children led by Laura O'Toole and Caitríona were advancing across the schoolyard towards them.

'I think they're looking for you Pin,' said Tony Ryan.

'What now?' moaned Jim.

He soon found out. In a few seconds he was surrounded by an excited crowd of children. Laura O'Toole seemed to be in charge of the demonstration.

'There's a picture of someone you know in the paper,' crowed Laura, smiling in a way that said she was going to enjoy watching him squirming. Then she handed the newspaper cutting to Jim.

He really didn't know what to expect. When he saw Pin's startled little face staring out from the photograph, he was astounded. He stood gazing at it while his head swam and his knees began to tremble. The group around him grew quiet. Something in Jim's face frightened them. At last he looked up from the photo. He ignored Laura O'Toole but he fixed his eyes on Caitríona. Her triumphant grin melted away. There was more than fury in that look. There was deep hurt and astonishment as well. Jim said nothing to her but Caitríona knew for certain that she had made an enormous mistake.

'Caitríona says that's Pin,' Laura announced loudly, 'and she has more photos at home.'

Caitríona didn't speak.

Jim looked down at the photo again and remained silent for quite a while. Everyone was watching him, waiting. Then he did the only thing he could do. He handed the photo back to Laura. 'Of course,' he said. 'That's Pin all right. He's a terrible show-off and very addicted to chocolate biscuits. He's one of the two dozen I told you about. The others are called Bin, Din, Fin, Gin, Hin, Kin, Nin, Rin, Sin, Tin, Vin, Zin and so on. They often dance jigs and reels up and down the back garden in the moonlight but they're not very good at spelling as you can see from the letter.'

Some of the crowd laughed. Others grumbled in frustration. Could this be real? Was he making fun of them?

Laura O'Toole felt her glory slipping away but she wasn't going to let Jim escape without causing him as much trouble as possible. 'Is Caitríona still raving then?' she asked, eyeing him craftily. Everyone knew she was challenging him to deny his sister's story.

Jim glanced at Caitríona. Then he looked Laura in the eye and said, 'Not as much as you are.'

Everyone laughed loudly. Before Laura could reply the bell rang, the teacher in charge of the yard began to walk towards them and the group broke up.

Caitríona ran all the way home from school without speaking to anyone. By the time Jim got home she had locked herself in her room. Mrs Doran was in the next-door neighbour's house and Eileen was drinking coffee in the kitchen.

'Was Caitríona in trouble at school?' she asked.

'What makes you think that?' replied Jim.

'Well, she banged in here, threw her bag on the floor, scowled at me, snatched up the bag again, dashed upstairs and locked her bedroom door. That kind of trouble.'

'Oh, we had a sort of disagreement,' sighed Jim. 'Don't worry. I'm going to sort it out.'

'I suggest you do it before Mam gets back,' said Eileen.

Jim picked up yesterday's *Daily Dawn* and headed up to his bedroom. Pin was standing on the window-sill behind the curtains, gazing out at the back garden in the fading evening light.

'Hello Jim,' he said quietly. 'I have a feeling that something is going to happen soon.'

'You're dead right about that,' replied Jim. 'Just look at this.' He switched on the bedroom light and held the newspaper up to Pin's face. 'Explain that away if you can.'

Pin seemed strangely calm as if the whole thing didn't matter. 'All right,' he murmured. 'It was my fault again. I went down to the kitchen during the night and your sister saw me. She flashed something in my face.'

Jim had intended eating the head off Pin but there was something sad about the look on his face and the quietness of his voice that made Jim hold back. 'Pin, do you never learn anything from all the trouble you get into?' he said. 'She took photographs of you. Now everyone in school knows about you. Not only that, but half the country will have seen your picture and read Cat's letter. Do you understand what that means? This is real trouble.'

Pin looked steadily at Jim for a second. 'The advice of the Seniors is that when big trouble comes you should keep calm and think! Now, the first thing we must do is talk to Caitríona.'

'I'm about to do that,' replied Jim grimly.

'Take it easy,' warned Pin. 'Just invite her in to see me. We haven't met properly yet.'

Jim knocked on Caitríona's door.

'Go away,' said a muffled voice.

'I won't go away,' replied Jim. 'I've got to talk to you. Open the door.'

The key turned in the lock and the door opened. As Jim stepped in Caitríona turned away and stood looking out the window with her back to him.

Jim closed the door behind him and stared at her in silence, not knowing how to begin. He saw the scrambled rubic cube on the shelf and noticed that the jigsaw was no longer on display.

'You are really horrible,' muttered Caitríona without turning round.

'And you are a total idiot!' exploded Jim. 'Do you realise what you've done?'

Caitríona turned on him angrily. 'I wouldn't have done anything if you weren't a liar and a mean cheat!' she shouted.

'Keep your voice down,' growled Jim. 'You've done

enough damage already.'

'What damage?' Caitríona asked sullenly.

'Telling everyone about him of course,' snapped Jim.

'And what's the harm in that?' persisted Caitríona. 'Why can't you show him to other people? Why must he be yours alone? Does he have a Private Property sign on him?'

'Oh come off it!' snapped Jim. 'You're not as stupid as that. What do you think they'll do to him? He'll be a performing monkey on TV — a freak for the world to gape at. They'll force him to tell them about his own people and then he'll never be able to get back there again. He'll live in misery for the rest of his life and that's a lot of misery because he could live for up to a thousand years. That's if they let him live. They'll probably want to do medical tests on him, stick needles in him, cut him open. You've ruined everything...'

His voice trailed off. He was almost crying.

'I'm sorry,' whispered Caitríona.

Jim stared at her. He hadn't expected her to apologise. 'I'm sorry too,' he said and he meant it. 'Pin wants to talk to you. We've got to work something out.'

Now that the moment she had longed for had actually come, Caitríona felt nervous. How could she face this extraordinary person after causing him so much trouble? What on earth was she going to say to him? She followed Jim into his bedroom feeling like a criminal entering a court.

Pin was standing beside Jim's bedside lamp. When he saw Caitríona he raised his hat and bowed gracefully.

'It is a pleasure to meet you, Caitríona,' he said.

Caitríona gazed at his perfect face with its twinkling eyes and at the small slender fingers that held his hat and was overcome by the sheer wonder of him. She bowed politely back to him. 'Hello Pin,' she said. He was looking at her very intently. Caitríona felt awkward. 'Thank you for fixing my bird and my music box,' she added. 'You must be very clever.'

'Not clever enough,' replied Pin with a regretful smile. 'My efforts at being helpful often have the opposite effect, I fear. I seem to have left a trail of disasters behind me as usual.'

'I haven't helped much either,' admitted Caitríona. 'I'm sorry about the other night.'

'My fault again,' sighed Pin. 'I was misbehaving.'

'You're a fantastic dancer,' said Caitríona.

'Thank you,' replied Pin, beaming with pleasure.

'If you two have had enough of admiring each other,' remarked Jim drily, 'we have an emergency to deal with.'

'Quite right as usual,' agreed Pin. 'Let us put our heads together and deal with the problem.'

Pin sat cross-legged on Jim's pillow while the children sat on the bed opposite him.

'Tell me how they reacted at school,' began Pin.

Caitríona told the story of what had happened and Jim took over when she reached the schoolyard scene. Pin didn't interrupt but nodded and 'hmmed' from time to time.

'From what you've told me,' he said when the children were finished, 'your friends are still not sure if I'm real or not. If no further evidence of my existence appears, they'll likely forget the whole thing.'

'But there are bound to be a lot more questions before that happens,' objected Caitríona. 'What are we to say? I don't want them all to think I was telling lies again.'

'You don't have to say it isn't true,' replied Pin. 'Tell them that you've both agreed not to speak about it any more because it only causes trouble. They'll be annoyed with you for a while but they'll get over it when some new distraction comes along. I'd be more concerned with the reaction of the adults. What about your teachers?'

'Nobody has told them yet,' replied Jim.

'Let's hope it stays that way,' said Pin. 'What about your Mum and Dad?'

'They haven't said anything so far,' replied Jim.

'They often don't get around to reading all the paper,' added Caitríona, 'so if no one else tells them, they may never know.'

'Someone is bound to tell them,' objected Jim.

'Did you put your full name and address on the original letter?' asked Pin.

'No, I didn't,' Caitríona answered.

'Good,' said Pin. 'The *Daily Dawn* is the real danger. If they get no response to the article they may just forget about it. If they get a good reaction they'll want to follow it up. Let's hope they don't try to trace you.'

☙

But the *Daily Dawn* did. Bob Whaley had faxed the story to Boston and New York. The head of a Japanese factory in Boston that made plastic leprechauns and garden gnomes, phoned Mike Kelly. He wanted to buy the sole rights for a whole new line of leprechauns based on Pin. He wanted to know if the story was true and he was particularly keen to get a photo of 'That sweet little coleen' who sent in the letter. She would be great for publicity. That very evening two American journalists walked into the offices of the *Daily Dawn*. They had been in Dublin covering an EC meeting about trade between Europe and America. Their bosses had decided that their readers would be more interested in the 'Little People' than in politicians' speeches and had ordered them to find out about the story and get some pictures for themselves. Three reporters from the national papers had heard where the Americans were going and decided to tag along with them for the fun.

Mike Kelly got on the phone to trace the mysterious 'Catroona'. Then Alan Cowan, the *Daily Dawn's* sports photographer came in. He had a daughter in Caitríona's school and she had come home with the story of the scene in the schoolyard. After a quick phone-call to the Cowan home, the editor of the *Daily Dawn* had Caitríona's full name and her address. Bob Whaley phoned RTE and arranged for a television crew to call to the offices of the *Daily Dawn* the following morning.

'Didn't I tell you?' Bob laughed as he shook Mike's hand. 'This little fellow is going to be really big!'

Everyone laughed. Tomorrow they would play 'Hunt-the-Leprechaun'.

13   Pin's Best Trick

The following morning Jim awoke to the sound of music. Pin was standing in the middle of the window-sill, holding the curtains open while he gazed out at the back garden. The early sunlight shone on his face, turning his curly hair into a golden halo as he sang softly:

'Di lonri noni mina lana,
Nira san, nira san.
Lo lorno foro dara mana,
Doro nan, doro nan.'

It was like a hymn to the morning sunrise and made Jim think of springtime with daffodils glowing in the shadow of the sycamore tree at the end of the garden. As he lay quietly listening to the liquid beauty of the melody, it occurred to him that it was exactly one week since Pin had appeared in his bedroom. Somehow it seemed much longer. A lot had happened in that week. A lot had changed.

Pin turned and saw Jim looking at him. 'Good morning,

young giant,' he called.

'Good morning ancient music man,' replied Jim. 'That was a beautiful song. What do the words mean?'

'Ah!' sighed Pin and a shadow crossed his face. 'It is forbidden to teach the language to outsiders.'

'Don't tell me,' grumbled Jim. 'It's the law of the Seniors.'

'Exactly,' agreed Pin.

There was a moment of silence between them.

'There is one thing I should mention,' Pin said heavily. 'I shall soon be leaving you.'

Jim was taken by surprise. He had become so used to having Pin around that he'd forgotten he would have to return to his own people. 'How do you know?' he asked.

'I can feel them,' replied Pin. 'They are coming nearer.'

There was a soft knock on the door. Jim sat up quickly. Surely they couldn't be that near! 'Who is it?' he called.

'It's me — Caitríona!'

'Come in,' said Jim, feeling relieved.

Caitríona appeared carrying a tray. She closed the door behind her. Then she set the tray down on the bed. She had brought breakfast for everyone. There were two glasses of freshly squeezed orange juice for herself and Jim and a thimbleful for Pin. She had crushed some cornflakes into an egg cup for Pin's cereal and added milk and sugar. There was a tiny spoon from her old doll's tea-set for Pin to use. She had brought Weetabix for Jim because he preferred it and she had muesli for herself.

'I thought we might as well have as much time as we can together,' she said by way of explanation. She was half-embarrassed by her own thoughtfulness.

Jim was wondering if his sister had become a mind-reader. How else could she have known that their time together was limited?

'This is magnificent!' exclaimed Pin, as he finished his juice.

'As good as a chocolate biscuit?' laughed Caitríona.

'Almost,' replied Pin through a mouthful of cornflakes.

'Abracadabra!' cried Caitríona and she produced a chocolate biscuit from her pocket.

'I think your sister is magic,' said Pin turning to Jim.

Looking at the two of them together, Jim wondered why he had been so keen to keep them apart. After they had discussed their worries and plans the night before, they had spent several hours going back over everything that had happened since Pin had arrived and they had laughed themselves sore over incidents that had enraged them at the time. It was the longest complete conversation that Jim had ever had with Caitríona without an argument and he was beginning to see a side of his sister that he hadn't noticed before.

'What are we going to do today?' she said, when they had finished eating.

'I'd like to explore the back garden,' suggested Pin.

Just then they heard Mrs Doran's voice calling, 'Caitríona!'

Pin vanished under the duvet while Caitríona opened the door and answered, 'In here, Mum.'

Mary Doran put her head around the door and stared in surprise. 'What's going on here?' she asked.

'Oh, I thought Jim might like his breakfast in bed,' explained Caitríona.

Her mother looked at her as if she had gone mad. 'Really?' she murmured. 'How nice.'

There was a moment of awkward silence.

'Your father and I are going shopping,' continued Mary Doran, looking doubtfully from Caitríona to Jim. 'Eileen is going to the hairdresser's. I want the two of you to behave while we're out. No fighting. Do the wash-up. Tidy and vacuum your bedrooms. If you're busy you won't get into mischief. If there's any trouble there'll be no pocket money today. Understand?'

'Of course,' replied Jim.

'There'll be no trouble,' promised Caitríona.

When the others had gone, Jim and Caitríona decided they'd better finish their work before they did anything else. They got washed and dressed, then they headed downstairs to the kitchen. It was great to be able to move about the house without having to keep Pin hidden and he celebrated his freedom by doing cartwheels along the hall.

Matsa was in the kitchen. She got quite excited when she spotted Pin. Jim put her outside the back door with a saucer of milk to keep her happy but she sat there miaowing at them to let her in.

Caitríona did the washing and Jim the drying. Pin was supposed to be helping to dry the cutlery but he spent most of his time staring out the window at the back garden. Then Matsa leaped up onto the window-sill and tried to get at Pin through the glass. Pin had great fun pretending to tickle Matsa's nose while she pawed the window trying to scratch his hand.

Then the doorbell rang. When Jim opened the front door he almost fell down with shock. There were four men standing on the doorstep. One had a camera and the other three carried notebooks and pens. Behind them the driveway was blocked by a white van marked RTE. Two men were unloading a television camera from it while a third carried the lights. There was a crowd of journalists on the lawn.

As soon as they saw Jim their cameras flashed and everyone began shouting questions. Jim said nothing. He stared at them for a second, then he slammed the door, turned the key in the lock and dashed back into the kitchen.

'What's wrong?' asked Caitríona when she saw his face. 'Who was it?'

'Just half the journalists in the country,' replied Jim. 'They even have a TV crew out there.'

'Oh no!' exclaimed Caitríona, turning pale.

The doorbell was ringing again. Then the letter-box rattled and an American voice shouted down the hall, 'Hey kids. We only want to talk to you. Come on out. Your photos will be in the paper and we'll even give you money — big money.'

'This is much worse than I feared,' said Jim. 'What are we going to do?'

Pin turned away from the window. He looked very serious but completely calm. 'We are not going to panic,' he said in a clear, commanding voice. 'Steady yourselves. I can deal with these people. Will you trust me one last time?'

Jim and Caitríona looked anxiously at each other and then at Pin.

'Oh, all right,' agreed Jim. 'I trust you. I just hope you know what you're doing, because I don't.'

'Right, then,' said Pin, jumping down from the window-sill. 'Jim, go and get the jacket you were wearing in school last Monday and put it on.'

Jim opened the kitchen door and went into the hallway. Someone had his finger pressed against the doorbell and others were hammering on the door. As Jim took his jacket from the cupboard under the stairs, Bob Whaley looked in through the letterbox and saw him.

'Come on kid,' he shouted. 'Give us a break. How does ten thousand dollars pocket money sound to you? Look, here's something for starters.' He pushed a crumpled ten pound note through the letterbox.

'They're completely crazy,' muttered Jim as he hurried back into the kitchen.

'If we don't do something quickly they'll break the door down,' said Caitríona.

'Now,' continued Pin. 'While you two were at school I took the opportunity of watching a good deal of television. I believe in cases like this, it is the custom to hold a press conference.'

'Are you mad?' squeaked Jim. 'They'll fry and boil you and have you for their breakfast!'

'Oh no they won't,' replied Pin. 'After our discussion, I spent most of last night thinking this out and it will work. Now listen carefully.'

Within a few minutes Pin had explained his plan and made sure the children knew exactly what to do. Jim put his jacket on and placed Pin in the breast pocket with the flap covering his head. Then he locked the door between the kitchen and the sittingroom and organised the furniture as well as he could.

Meanwhile Caitríona ran upstairs to her bedroom and opened the window. Immediately there were cries of, 'There she is! It's the leprechaun girl!'

'Listen!' shouted Caitríona at the top of her voice. 'We can't possibly talk to you while you're making all that noise and would the ignorant person who is ringing our doorbell please have the manners to stop.'

The people below weren't used to being spoken to like this. They quietened down and the doorbell stopped ringing.

'Now,' called Caitríona. 'We're going to hold a press conference. We will answer all your questions and you can take as many photos as you want as long as you are well-mannered and don't make a row. Otherwise we'll call the police. Do you agree?'

'Of course, dear,' answered Mike Kelly. 'That's all we want anyhow.'

'Good,' said Caitríona. 'Wait a moment and I'll let you in
— and no rushing or pushing please.'

'She's like a bloomin' school mistress,' muttered Bob
Whaley as Caitríona shut the window.

'This isn't America,' retorted Mike. 'Take it easy and we'll
get what we want without all the fuss and with a lot less
expense as well.'

Caitríona opened the front door and the journalists and
photographers filed in. She even made some of them put out
their cigarettes before they were let into the house.

Jim was waiting for them in the sittingroom and he di-
rected them to their chairs. Soon the room was quite crowded
and some of the reporters had to sit on the floor.

'Where's the leprechaun?' shouted Bob Whaley. He was in
a bad temper. He hated being ordered about, especially by
children and he felt he'd been made to look foolish in front
of the others. He was also very annoyed at having to abandon
an expensive cigar on the doorstep.

'Yeah, let's have some action,' murmured some of the
others.

'Just a moment,' said Jim taking control of the situation and
listening carefully to the whispered instructions from his
breast pocket. 'We're going to do this properly, or not at all.
First of all I want the reporters to call out their names and the
papers they're from. Then we'll take the questions in order.'

'Where did you get these kids from?' growled Bob Whaley
to Mike Kelly. 'They sound like they want to run the White
House.'

'Maybe they should,' retorted Mike. 'They might do something for the little people of the world! Ha!'

'Very funny,' scowled Bob.

While the television people were running cables in
through the windows and setting up lights, the reporters

identified themselves. There was Sylvie Rakish from the *Sunday Globe*, who was famous for making up stories about people if the truth about them wasn't interesting enough. Sylvie was a little man, less than five feet tall. He had gone bald when he was twenty-eight and his big 'secret' was the hairpiece he wore to keep himself looking young. Nobody was supposed to know about it and he was very touchy about people even hinting that his hair looked peculiar.

Next to Sylvie was Archie Carper of the *Daily Freeman*. He was a tall grey-haired man with a thin sour face and tufts of grey hair growing out of his ears. He was an impatient but honest journalist who had no time for Sylvie.

Behind these two sat Honor Worthington of the *High Times*. She regarded all other journalists as less intelligent than herself. No matter what she was writing about she used words that were hard to understand. She was especially fond of hyphens and French words that she typed in italics. She wasn't in very good humour that morning because she felt that this story wasn't important enough for her.

Beside Honor sat the dozy Christy Mockler from the *Weekly Watcher*, a paper famous for its misprints and spelling mistakes. They even got Christy's name wrong so that he sometimes appeared as Chrusty Muckler and once as Crisp Muncher.

In the back row sat Brad Swinger from the *New York Yippee*. He believed that all press conferences should end with a party and he was beginning to fear that this one might not.

Beside him sat the silent Clint Harding from Chicago who was wondering if there was a criminal side to the story. Next to him was grumpy Bob Whaley, while Mike Kelly sat nearest the door.

As each journalist identified himself, the others passed jokey comments or chatted among themselves about the newspaper business.

Inside Jim's pocket, Pin's sharp ears picked up every word they said and his keen eyes watched them through the button-hole. He had seen Sylvie and Archie on the television during the week. He was ready for anything that might happen.

'Now we'll take the questions, starting with the most important paper,' announced Jim.

'Thank you,' purred Honor Worthington as she stood up with a self-satisfied smile. 'I've heard that you've got dozens of these little people and I'd like to know...'

'Hold on a minute,' cut in Archie Carper. 'What makes you think you're the most important one here?'

'Oh come now!' boomed Honor in her grandest voice. 'Surely that is perfectly obvious.'

'Should I put a hyphen between perfectly and obvious?' drawled Christy Mockler, pretending to write her words down. The others laughed. Honor flushed with annoyance.

'Never mind her honour,' said Arche Carper. 'Where's the little man?'

Everyone looked at Jim and Caitríona.

'Well,' repeated Archie. 'Where's the leprechaun?'

'He's sitting beside you!' shouted the voice of Bob Whaley.

Little Sylvie Rakish was sitting beside Archie. He sprang to his feet in astonishment. 'Just who are you calling a leprechaun?' he thundered, his face bright red with fury.

Bob gaped at him in amazement. 'I — I didn't say a word,' he stammered. He was just as surprised as Sylvie.

'Fat liar,' muttered Sylvie.

'Good man, Pin,' whispered Jim. 'Keep it up.'

'You mind who you're calling a liar,' growled Whaley.

'Pah!' snorted Sylvie, turning his back on the Whale. Then he pointed a long crooked finger at Caitríona and said, 'How much did Whaley and Kelly pay you to make up this story?'

'How dare you suggest we bribed the child!' protested Mike Kelly.

'Sylvie thinks we're all like himself,' remarked Archie Carper sourly.

'I'm just after the real facts of the story,' insisted Sylvie.

'Very likely,' called Bob Whaley's voice. 'Everyone knows that your stories are as real as your fake hair.'

There was a stunned silence. Sylvie's mouth fell open. So did Bob's. It was exactly what the Whale had been thinking but he definitely hadn't said it out loud. Sylvie was white with rage. He turned on Bob Whaley with trembling lips.

'You — you — ' he spluttered, almost choking with fury. 'You fat, over-fed, big-headed, whiskey-gulping Yank!'

'Now that's what I call hyphens,' chuckled Christy Mockler, winking at Honor Worthington.

Bob Whaley was on his feet, shaking his fat fist at Sylvie. 'Now you watch it, Tiny,' he threatened, 'or I'll knock some manners into that false head of yours.'

Sylvie flung down his pen and notebook and tried to climb over Christy Mockler to get at the Whale.

'Hey, watch where you're putting your feet!' protested Christy.

'Oh shut up, you miserable little misprint!' raged Sylvie.

Christy pushed Sylvie off him so that he staggered back and fell on the floor. Sylvie leaped to his feet, fairly dancing with rage. 'Let me at the fat fool!' he shrieked.

Then Pin spoke, using Jim's voice. 'If you want to fight you can do it outside. You're not going to wreck my sittingroom.'

'Right!' shouted Bob Whaley, glaring at Sylvie. 'Outside, you miserable leprechaun.'

'I'll leprechaun you,' screamed Sylvie.

The two of them rushed from the room and out the front

door where they collided head-on with Stewart Crowe, the RTE special reporter, who had just arrived. In a few moments the sittingroom had emptied, as everyone crowded out into the garden to watch the fight. Caitríona skipped into the hall and shut the front door firmly.

Pin's head popped out of Jim's pocket, with a wide wicked grin on his face. 'How did I do?' he smirked.

'Brilliant,' replied Jim. 'Now what?'

'Take me out to your back garden,' ordered Pin. 'It's important,' he added, seeing the puzzled look on Jim's face.

Once they were outside the back door, Jim checked that Matsa wasn't about, then he set Pin down on the doorstep and the children sat beside him.

'I realise this is rather sudden,' began Pin, 'but it's time for me to go.'

'Oh no!' gasped Caitríona. 'But we've hardly — '

'I know,' agreed Pin. 'It's not my choice of time, but this is the moment.'

'How do you know?' asked Jim.

'I can hear the Troop Horns calling,' replied Pin. 'Listen.'

Jim and Caitríona listened. At first they could only hear the angry noises from the fight in the front garden. Then they began to hear another sound, faint and echoing as of horns blowing a long way off. Gradually it grew clearer. It was a rich sweet sound. They felt it was calling them to come away to beautiful, quiet places long since forgotten by the noisy fussy world.

'Goodbye, young giants,' said Pin. 'Be kind to each other. You are good people and I will not forget you. I'm sorry for causing so much trouble.'

'You're a good person too, Pin,' said Jim. 'We'll always remember you. Thanks for everything.'

Caitríona stretched out her hand to Pin. He gazed at her

gravely. Then he removed his hat and leaning forward he kissed the end of her finger. 'Goodbye, my lady,' he said.

'Goodbye Pin,' whispered Caitríona.

The horns sounded quite near now. Pin replaced his hat.

'Do not follow me,' he said. 'The Troop might not understand that you are my friends and they can be dangerous.'

He leaped from the step and sped off across the lawn, almost hidden by the long grass. Then the children spotted a movement by the hedge at the end of the garden and suddenly a troop of small figures appeared. They were dressed in green, brown and grey so that they were almost invisible against the hedge but the children noticed a glint of polished horns and weapons. Two of the troop hurried forward to meet Pin and escort him back to the others. Jim and Caitríona could see him talking excitedly and waving his hands as the troop gathered round him. Then they all turned to face the children and each one raised his right arm in salute to Pin's friends. The children waved back. Then the whole troop stepped into the hedge and vanished.

Jim and Caitríona stood staring at the garden in silence for quite a while.

'Well,' sighed Jim at last. 'He's gone.'

'What do we do now?' asked Caitríona.

The noise of battle still sounded from the front of the house.

'I suppose we'd better see what's happening out there,' said Jim. 'I'm afraid Pin has left us to tidy up the mess, as usual.'

They went inside to the sittingroom and looked out the front window. The scene in the garden was unbelievable. Archie Carper had just pushed Christy Mockler's head into the hedge and he was trying to shove the rest of him in after it. In the middle of the lawn, Bob Whaley had Sylvie Rakish by the throat. It looked as if the Whale was trying to shake his head off. Sylvie's head stayed on but his hair didn't. The wig flew off and sailed across the lawn into the flower bed. Matsa saw it landing. She pounced on it and dashed off with the hair-piece dangling from her mouth like a blow-dried rat.

All the others were cheering and waving their hands, while the cameras flashed and Stewart Crowe stood on the wall giving an excited commentary as if he was at a football match. The Dorans' neighbours gathered in their gardens to watch the display. Most of them thought they were shooting a scene for a comedy film.

Then a squad car sped up to the gate. Four Gardai sprang out and rushed into the garden. It was at that moment that Tom and Mary Doran arrived back with Eileen.

'Oh-oh!' said Jim. 'This is where things get complicated.'

Mrs Doran couldn't have looked more astounded if a herd of elephants had been holding a disco in her garden. Tom Doran ordered Stewart Crowe down from the wall. He spoke briefly to the Garda Sergeant, then he helped pull Chris Mockler out of the hedge. At this point an ambulance arrived. Eileen helped her mother into the house.

'There'd better be a very good explanation for all this, that's all I'm saying,' wailed Mary Doran.

'There Mam,' soothed Eileen. 'Just sit down and I'll make you a cup of tea.'

The front door slammed and Tom Doran strode in. 'Where are Jim and Caitríona?' he asked.

'We're in here,' called Jim.

'Now we're for it,' whispered Caitríona.

Their father stepped into the sittingroom and closed the door behind him. 'Are you two all right?' he asked.

'Yes, we're fine,' replied Jim. He was surprised that his father wasn't already roaring at him.

'Right then,' said Tom. 'Sit down there and start explaining. I couldn't get any sense out of that lot of lunatics out there.'

Jim and Caitríona glanced at each other, then Jim began.

'Well, Dad, it all started exactly a week ago. I know this may be difficult to believe, but I woke up and found a little man sitting on the floor of my bedroom. His name was Pin. Well, that's what I called him but his real name — '

Then Jim stopped talking because a very strange look had come over his father's face and a light gleamed in his eye that the chldren had never seen before.

'Ah!' exclaimed Tom Doran. 'Pinbindimdominilli!'

Jim and Caitríona were astounded. They gaped open-mouthed at their father.

'That explains everything,' continued Tom. 'It's a wonder the Seniors let him out again.'

'Dad!' exclaimed Jim. 'You know him!'

'Well, sort of,' said their father. 'He caused your grandfather a lot of trouble long ago. I only met him for a few hours.'

'But you never told us,' said Caitríona.

'Of course I didn't,' replied her father. 'You wouldn't have believed me. Besides, it's the Great Law, isn't it?'

'How did you and Grandad come to know him?' asked Jim.

'That's a very long story,' smiled Tom.

'Oh come on Dad,' protested Caitríona. 'You have to tell us, now that we know about him.'

'All right,' agreed Tom. 'I'll tell you my story after you tell me yours. But first of all we have one of Pin's nice little messes to sort out and I see my friend Sergeant Casey coming up the garden path.'

'Is Pin likely to come back?' asked Caitríona as her father stood up to answer the doorbell.

'If he stayed for a week he must have liked you,' replied Tom, 'so I'm rather afraid he will.'

'Yes!' exclaimed Jim and Caitríona together.

Tom Doran laughed as he left the room.

'I wonder why Pin didn't tell us he knew Dad?' said Caitríona.

'We can ask him that if he ever comes back,' replied Jim. 'He probably thought it was the best trick of all.'

&

The riot in Dorans' garden was quickly over. No one was actually injured and everyone apologised in the Garda station. The idea of a group of journalists out searching for a leprechaun amused Sergeant Casey so much that he decided not to charge anyone, as long as they kept the story to themselves and promised not to annoy Tom Doran any further. Realising they would all look foolish if the story got published and wanting to avoid being brought to court, the journalists all agreed. So there were no photos of Jim or Caitríona in the papers the next day and no further mention of Pin either.

At school Jim and Caitríona refused to talk about Pin to anyone. Whenever they were asked about him they simply said, 'He's gone away again.' After a few weeks the story was forgotten about. Caitríona and Deirdre Nolan remained steady friends and were all the happier for that. Without Masher Moran, the bully group melted away and Mondays were no longer a problem for Jim now that Attila was gone.

Jim and Caitríona had to agree that Pin had certainly changed things for the better, even though he was a trickster to the very end.

Also by Cormac MacRaois

The Battle Below Giltspur

'Riveting fantasy .. a fast-moving tale where no words are wasted. From the awakening of the scarecrow Glasán, the story moves at an ever-increasing pace with strange incidents, frightening gatherings and terrifying sequences in rapid succession ... Absolutely brilliant ... exciting, funny and adventurous.' *Books Ireland.*

Dance of the Midnight Fire

'Full of magic, of the mysteries of the enchanted forest, of wolves and dripping shadows and of the strange and dangerous dance of the midnight fire.' *Cork Examiner.*

Lightning over Giltspur

It is Hallowe'en, the most menacing and magical time of year. Niamh and Daire are attacked on the road, sheep are savaged by dogs, the scarecrow is stolen, Daire is accused of smoking and Niamh of lying and stealing .... The Morrigan and an army of Shadow Slaves have returned to Giltspur — to seek revenge ...